CUT ROAD

stories

ESSENTIAL PROSE SERIES 197

**Canada Council Conseil des Arts
for the Arts du Canada**

**ONTARIO ARTS COUNCIL
CONSEIL DES ARTS DE L'ONTARIO**
an Ontario government agency
un organisme du gouvernement de l'Ontario

Canadä

Guernica Editions Inc. acknowledges the support of the Canada Council for
the Arts and the Ontario Arts Council. The Ontario Arts Council is an
agency of the Government of Ontario.

We acknowledge the financial support of the Government of Canada.

CUT ROAD

stories

BRENT VAN STAALDUINEN

GUERNICA
EDITIONS
TORONTO · CHICAGO · BUFFALO · LANCASTER (U.K.)
2022

Guernica Founder: Antonio D'Alfonso

Editor: Michael Mirolla
Interior design: David Moratto
Cover design: Rafael Chimicatti
Guernica Editions Inc.
287 Templemead Drive, Hamilton, ON L8W 2W4
2250 Military Road, Tonawanda, N.Y. 14150-6000 U.S.A.
www.guernicaeditions.com

Distributors:
Independent Publishers Group (IPG)
600 North Pulaski Road, Chicago IL 60624
University of Toronto Press Distribution (UTP)
5201 Dufferin Street, Toronto (ON), Canada M3H 5T8
Gazelle Book Services, White Cross Mills
High Town, Lancaster LA1 4XS U.K.

First edition.
Printed in Canada.

Legal Deposit—First Quarter
Library of Congress Catalog Card Number: 2021949429
Library and Archives Canada Cataloguing in Publication
Title: Cut road : stories / Brent van Staalduinen.
Names: van Staalduinen, Brent, 1973- author.
Identifiers: Canadiana (print) 20210359013 | Canadiana (ebook) 20210359021
| ISBN 9781771837255 (softcover) | ISBN 9781771837262 (EPUB)
Classification: LCC PS8643.A598 C88 2022 | DDC C813/.6—dc23

For Kirsten, Dennis, and Sharon

CONTENT

SKINKS

JESSE DOESN'T LIKE it when I call him Dad, but I still do. *Two things*, he'll say. *One, your dad left a long time ago. Two, although you don't want to say he's your dad, he still is. I'm not. Clear?*

Clear, I'll say. But it's not clear, really. Jesse feels like a dad. He always finds ways to make me laugh, even when I'm sad. If dads aren't supposed to do that, then who is? Then he'll say, *Clear as mud?* I'll say that back to him, too. Clear as mud. Even though mud's not clear—it's muddy.

Jesse always ends his stories the same, with Two Things and Clear as Mud. Or he did, anyway. He's in the hospital now with all these machines that Mom says do pretty much everything for him, so he can't tell me anything. Once, I asked him about why he ended stories that way. He put down his beer bottle, the one with the big green 50 on the side, looked at me and then off at the trees. He said, *They're leftovers from the Army—you have to make sure you're heard and understood.* It sounded like he was saying it to someone else. You know what I mean about that? When grownups talk to you and to someone else you can't see at the same time?

1

I have to talk more to my Mom now. She used to watch a whole lot more than she spoke. While Jesse rode me around on his shoulders or helped me build things in the dirt—I saw buildings and castles and cities but I think they were invisible to him—she'd just watch us play, leaning her long legs over the arms of the camping chair I liked to sit in when she wasn't home. She liked cold wine and a joint when she got home, not talking.

"Dills, I've said enough to last two lifetimes. Understand?"

"No," I said. "That sounds too long."

She said, "It does, doesn't it?" and laughed that good laugh she made when evening came and the sun was almost down.

Pastor Van Egmond smells like peppermint but his collars are always dirty. He comes by the hospital to chat with Mom often enough. With me and her already in Jesse's room, there's never anywhere for him to sit so he stands and talks, moving his hands around in his pockets like they can't stand that he's not sitting either. He hasn't opened his Bible this time—he just laid it down on the metal heating grate beneath the window—and hasn't since the first visit when he talked to her from it and she got so upset that she had to ask me to leave. Probably so I wouldn't hear her say bad things to the minister. "He thinks all the answers are in that book, Buddy," she said later. I think it's confusing where I'm supposed to find the answers —grownups seem to stash them in all sorts of places.

Today they mostly talk about serious things. It's making Mom tired. I like it better when he tells stories about the other people in the church that make us laugh.

"Maybe I should talk to Wendell about it," he says.

Mom says, "Would you like that, Wendell?"

She's smiling because she knows what I'll say next.

"It's Dills, Mom."

"Right. Dills."

"You promised you'd call me that."

"You're right, I did."

"Anyway, I don't know if I'd like it," I say. "How can I know that?"

"Well, it's settled then," she says to the pastor, still smiling at me.

The pastor isn't happy about the way we're making jokes. He says, "Jesse and I go way back. He'd want me to help."

"You and I go way back too. Look how that all turned out."

"This is serious, Vicky."

She stops smiling. "I know it's serious. But that was years ago, when you both loved getting into trouble. He's different now."

"Well, how'd he end up in here, then, eh? We all saw the same things. Some of us know better than to get into fights over the stupid things people say."

"I told you what Jesse said before he went under."

"You did, but the police and the newspapers say different."

They stop talking for a bit. Right after Jesse's accident, the police were here even before Mom and I arrived and needed to talk with her right away. Mom hid the next day's newspaper, and said I wouldn't like the way it made Jesse look, that it wasn't guilty until proven innocent but the other way around.

⟶

Jesse's favourite thing is the .22 rifle he keeps locked up in the cupboard. He uses it to get the squirrels away from Mom's birdfeeder and the raccoons away from the garbage. He's so good at shooting, too. He always kills the squirrels with a single shot to the eye and never misses. The raccoons squall like they're so mad when he shoots them in the ass—that's what Jesse says, I'm not allowed to say ass—and he always laughs and laughs. The raccoons are stupid, though, because they always come back.

If there aren't any animals to shoot at he sets up things like cans and bottles all the way across the yard. We live in an old house where you can see a farmer's field on one side and more houses on the other. I like to play in the field when Jesse and I aren't shooting cans or talking. He likes the field, too, says that it's Clear Downrange and he can shoot without worrying. His breathing changes when he shoots like that. He lays down on the grass and slows it down like he's sleeping or something, deep in and deep out and deep in and deep out and *SNAP!* he hits whatever he puts there.

A few weeks ago, before the hospital, we shared a root beer and set the can across the yard. Five shots, five sharp little holes. "Two things about shooting," he said. "One, don't forget to breathe. Two, it's not a gun, it's a rifle." He handed it to me and I looked through the holes. "Clear as mud," I said, trying to say it even before he could. Then I asked if we could shoot the brown beer bottles next time he had a 50, but he said we couldn't because he didn't want to leave little shards of glass everywhere for Mom to find later on.

He could shoot all day. And he did, sometimes.

It's hard to know when to laugh. Mom can be laughing one second and crying the next. "You'll understand when you get to know women," she said one day. I went out to see Jesse in the garage and he shook his head and said exactly the same thing, even though I hadn't told him what she'd said at all. It was crazy.

I'm just glad she laughs more than she cries, like there's some big house inside her that holds it all, but keeps the sadness in a bedroom while the happiness plays all over. It must be a big room, though, because the sadness got out once and she cried for a whole week. I wondered how much laughing she'd have to do to make up for it. She and Jesse had come home from the hospital. They wanted the doctors to check on the baby they'd just started telling everyone about. A new brother or sister for me. A few days before, Mom's aunt gave her a present, a box that was a strange colour, kind of like purple and pink all mixed up, and inside there were these tiny shirts and things that had superhero pictures all over them. Superman S's and Spiderman spiders and other cool stuff. Anyway, when Mom started crying, she cried so deep and hard that I knew that the baby died. So I tried to find that box to cheer her up but Jesse told me to stop looking. The clothes were too small, maybe. Babies wear crazy small clothing.

᠉

Talking to Jesse feels funny because he can't talk back, but a guy has to tell guy things to another guy. Like the little lizard I saw under the gurney in the hallway and how the nurse screamed and called the janitor, and how he just laughed and teased her about being scared of a little skink. I see them all over the place outside, but never knew what they were called.

"Skink," I say to Jesse. "It's a weird word but I like it."

I like it too, I imagine him saying back to me.

"I could go and try to catch it. To show you."

You'd do that for me?

"Of course I would, Dad."

All right, but don't hurt yourself.

I sprint into the hallway before he can correct me about calling him Dad. Even if it's in my mind, I still don't like it when he tells me not to.

᠉

"You disappeared," Mom says.

I don't always know where she is, but I can usually find her in the smoking area behind the hospital. The first day, she told me that this will be our Emergency

Assembling Area, but there aren't any emergencies so I just go there. It's a nice spot, fenced in and shady with picnic tables and a bucket filled with sand where the nurses and janitors put their cigarette butts. I sit beside her on the bench.

"The skink wasn't there anymore, so I came outside to find another one," I say.

"What skink?"

"It's a lizard."

"I know what it is, Dills. Which one?"

"The one in Dad's hallway—up there."

I point at a window way up the side of the hospital, but I'm just guessing. The building's made of this pink stone—I knew the stone but I forget now—and it's really bright in the sun.

"Jesse. Not Dad."

"I know, Mom."

I don't mind her saying it so much because I'm more used to it somehow, even though I wish she wouldn't. Like when you like a song but hear it too much and end up loving it without wanting to hear it.

"Did you get one?"

I hold up my empty hands. "Does it look like I got one, Sweetie?"

I say this in my big voice, the one I use to make her laugh. She does.

"Struck right out, eh?"

No, I had one over by that big tree but it got away, I want to say. But I don't—the stories where you lose things never make her laugh.

Instead, I say, "Yeah—I really wanted to show him one."

She gives me a side hug, with one arm. Says, "I know you did, Bud."

She smells like cigarettes and bread and something sweeter underneath. I wonder if she always smells so good, whether being at home and doing our normal things kind of covers it up until we come here. Inside the hospital it smells like chemicals and throw-up and out here there's no real smell at all except when someone is smoking.

⤳

"Where'd you grow up?"

A farm not too far from here, Jesse imagine-says.

"Did you like it on the farm?"

Hell, no. He says bad things in our pretend talks like he does in real life.

I ask, "Why not?"

Because it's a hard life. Farmers are poor.

"Mom says money isn't everything."

She's right, but it's pretty important.

"Did you learn to shoot on the farm?"

Yes. And no. I got much better at it later on.

"We've always lived in the city. I wish we could live out—"

No, you don't.

"But the city is so—"

One, be thankful your mom is raising you here. Two, stay in school so your choices are all yours, all right?

Mom and a police officer and one of the nice nurses come into the room before I can ask him to explain. I hate it when he talks in riddles even in pretend. The officer's hat is under his arm.

"Ma'am, I'm sorry, but things have changed," he says.

The nurse just holds some long, dangly things in her hand and looks at the floor.

"Go into the hall," Mom says to me.

"Why?" I ask. "I'm just talking to Dad—"

"Go, Dills. Now."

Well, I know that voice. I call it, Do Not Argue With Me Right Now Young Man. So I do, so fast I can't understand much of what Mom is saying to the police officer—but I can hear she's upset.

"Do you have to—my son's right outside—what the doctors said about—it just seems so cruel—"

She didn't ask me to close the door or anything, so I can still peek around. The police officer isn't responding to her, even though her voice is telling him to. I don't get why grownups get to ignore each other but they're always telling us to listen and pay attention. He nods at the nurse, who attaches the things in her hands to the bedframe and then ties up Jesse's wrists and ankles. Tight. So tight he couldn't do anything if he wanted, even go to the bathroom. I can't say anything, though, because they don't know I'm looking. Mom just sits in the chair and watches, and I want to go sit next to her.

⁊

The old man in the bed next to Jesse's doesn't talk. He's so skinny he couldn't even climb a rope, I don't think, but still has those strappy things they put on Jesse, too. There was no police officer there when the nurse did it a few days ago. The old man woke everyone up—me and Mom, I mean, not Jesse—when it was still really dark outside and was yelling all these crazy things. The nurse apologized and said it's been months since Henry acted out like this. He just looked scared, I thought, so why was it his fault? I went back to sleep almost right away, but I remember Mom getting up and whispering into Jesse's ear and smiling at him. I also remember me saying how much better it would be if we took Jesse home because there he could have his own room and he wouldn't need those straps like Henry does. And Mom's half laugh and her telling me how generous I am.

❧

"What's going on, Wendell?"

"Dills."

"Oh, right. Sorry."

"That's okay."

This is another funny conversation, the kind you seem to have all the time with grownups, like they can't remember anything. And where they don't really talk or listen to you, either. Pastor Van Egmond gets it wrong and makes me go through it every time—I think he should have a better memory to give all those long speeches every Sunday at church.

"I'm looking for skinks," I say.

He smiles, and suddenly it's like he's really looking at me. "They're a bugger to catch, as I recall."

And they really are, I think. Faster than anything I've

ever seen, even squirrels and birds. I'm hunting around the big trees on the grassy area behind the hospital. It's nice back here—there are benches and picnic tables and lots of places for people in wheelchairs to sit by themselves in the shade. Once, I saw a couple of teenagers get into an argument with a woman in hospital PJs and storm off. They went to a picnic table not too far away and started kissing and rolling all over each other while the woman shook her IV tubes and raised her fist but couldn't go after them. Their mom, maybe.

I ask, "You caught them?"

"Yep. But you have to trap them," Pastor Van Egmond says.

I give him my Uh-Huh This Better Be Good look.

"Skinks eat insects and their larvae—you use them as bait."

"Larvae?"

"Baby bugs."

"Oh."

"But don't grab them by the tail."

"Why not?"

"They'll leave it with you and get away."

"Will it grow back?"

"Yes, but kind of stumpy."

"Gross."

"Maybe I can help you catch one when I visit tomorrow."

"Maybe," I say.

"How are you doing with all of this?" he asks, his hand moving in big circles, like he's pointing at the whole hospital.

"I want Jesse to wake up."

"You like Jesse, don't you?"

Well, of course I do, I think. He shows me stuff and tells me secrets and treats me like he wants me to be around. And he's nice to Mom. But it's so obvious I don't say anything.

"If he wakes up—"

"*When* he wakes up," I say.

"—he probably won't be coming home with you and your Mom."

"Yes, he will. He told me—"

But I stop, because he might have said it in one of our pretend talks and I'm pretty sure the Pastor won't understand.

"He forgot how to look at people for who they really are, warts and all," Mom said once when I asked. "Warts and all," Jesse laughed. "You sure got your share with me, didn't you?" Then they kissed and Mom slapped his shoulder and told him he had beer breath. "Well, it's noon somewhere," he said.

"Jesse killed someone, Dills."

I say, "Mom said that it was an accident."

"It doesn't look that way."

But I just shake my head and tell him he's wrong. Mom says he was wrong for not marrying her and Dominic, my first dad, that he doesn't know people at all. You should let people who're having kids get married because sometimes dads can't handle it when they're not.

And I say, "You should be nice to Jesse because one, he told me he's staying around, and two, you're innocent until proven guilty."

I don't know where all that comes from—it just comes out. But I don't ask him if it's clear as mud. I just walk right away from him.

꣸

The skinks won't look at the bugs I've killed for them, ants and beetles and even a fly I can catch only because it's missing a wing. They run all around the box and the stick I can pull with a string but ignore the bugs in the white petri dish underneath. I was going to wait until tomorrow to build the trap but there were too many people in Jesse's room. I wanted to tell Mom about what I said to the pastor, but her eyes were red and she was crying and she asked if I could go and play and maybe come back later. The janitor gave me a white box that used to hold bandages, the string, and the petri dish. "They use lots of them in the lab," he said, "so they'll never miss just one."

I stand up and the skinks scatter to their holes and I'm by myself again. I stretch—I've been laying on the ground forever—and walk to the store across the street to buy a drink with the fiver—that's what Jesse calls them—Mom pressed into my hand. The lady behind the counter looks like she's never seen a guy work up a thirst before.

"You gonna drink all that?"

"Yep. All two litres," I say.

Good choice, I imagine Jesse saying. *Coke's my favourite too.*

The guy in the pet store next door is rearranging the window display. In an aquarium, I see lizards—bright green and brown and one that's almost black—sitting on branches, their tails dangling. There's a little tray with twisty little worms. One of the lizards zaps one with its tongue so fast it's like a blink and eats it whole.

"Meal worms," the guy says when I ask. "They're larvae."

"Baby bugs," I say.

He smiles. "Right."

❧

On the elevator, I remember the bottle of Coke and slap myself on the forehead. I left it on the pet store counter when the guy gave me some meal worms for free. You have to buy a hundred of them or more and I only needed a few. I was so excited I just left it there. I'm a little thirsty now, but the box under my arm is way more important. It only took a few minutes for the skinks to find the meal worms and I dropped the box on three of them all at once. The smallest of them has a little stumpy tail, just like Pastor Van Egmond said could happen.

"Are you all right?"

The old woman next to me is looking at me like I might explode. She has a black dress on, a big hat with dark feathers on it, and a bunch of white flowers under her arm. I hold up the white bandage box.

"Skinks," I say. "Lizards. Three of them. You feed them meal worms."

She flinches, sniffs, and looks at the numbers on the wall.

I hold the box to my ear, shake it a little until I hear the *skitch-skitch-skitch* of lizard feet. I almost tell the police officer who sits at a little desk next to Jesse's room about my skinks, but he looks down and gets back to writing something before I can. A tall, pale doctor with scruffy cheeks walks out with a nurse, speaking to her and checking his phone at the same time.

"I can't—they just talk so fast," Mom says to them as I come in.

She's leaning on the bed and holding Jesse's hand and looking at him. Pastor Van Egmond is there too with a hand on Mom's shoulder. I don't like that. His Bible is in the other, clutched against his side like it might fall at any second.

"You have some time," he says.

"It's what he'd want, I know, but I'm not sure I should make the decision."

"There's no one else, Victoria."

"I know."

A couple of metal clipboards and an uncapped, clear pen rest on the white bedspread. The machines next to Jesse are still doing their thing, hissing and whirring and sometimes making no sound at all. There are lights, numbers, words. I go to the other side of the bed and hold up the box and tell him about the three skinks and the meal worms and the forgotten Coke. It feels important and all comes out in a rush again, I don't know why, as I see the Pastor and my Mom look at each other and take a deep breath. Before I know it, I'm telling Dad about getting out a bottle of 50 and how we can take the bandage box behind our house and let the skinks out together and maybe they'll do just fine and I won't have to catch them again.

DRIFT, MAYBE FALL

BY SOME STROKE of the dumbest luck, the border is closed. No one knows who was at fault, the eighteen-wheeler heading north with a load of toilet paper or the logger moving south with forty tons of softwood. An instant of distraction and the two semis—the only rigs in sight—mashed it up. The fire, quick and hot, still burns. There's no wind, so the embers drift almost straight back down, coating Gretna in a layer of ash. The town smells like a campfire.

At the motel bar, a guy wearing an orange safety vest waves his beer around, slurring about how he'll still get paid for his time. Waxing philosophical.

"Not my fault," he says. "Company said to stay put, so—"

"It's the prairies, for God's sake," the bartender says. "There's a crossing every five clicks, east or west."

"Am I gonna complain?"

"Don't suppose you would, no."

"Universe sending me a message, maybe."

As the bartender rolls his eyes, a bell dings from the

kitchen window. He grunts, grabs the white Styrofoam takeout box and puts it in front of me.

"Dressing *on the side*," he says, with special contempt.

"Gotta cut back on the fat," I say. "Wife says so."

"Uh huh."

I drain the last of my beer and step back, ask if everything can go on my room bill. The guy in the orange vest snorts, makes a crack about The Maple Tree Motel not being the Hilton, but the bartender nods and prints off a receipt. I sign, click a toonie to the bar as a tip, and head towards the door.

I'm walking around the side of the building to get the truck, making perfect bootprints in the ash, before I stop myself and head back towards my room. Not used to parking the rig in the middle of a run. It's out back in the extended slots, stretched long in the shadows, and heavy with office supplies for Sioux Falls. Normally I'd have found another crossing and pushed through, but dispatch is all over my ass about downtime. Cab's not a sleeper so the regs say I have to find a bed.

A beige minivan swerves into the motel parking lot, slipping and sliding in the ash. I stop and watch, wondering if it can brake in time. A foot from the door, the van stops and a raccoon-eyed guy, young, steps out from behind the wheel, coating his white sneakers in sooty smudge.

"Stay here," he growls. There's a muffled cacophony from inside, a mashup of young voices. "I don't know, I'll ask, okay? Jesus."

The driver slams the door just as the clerk steps outside. Thick beard, checked shirt, looking like he'd rather be anywhere else.

She sits cross-legged on the stained carpet and I'm in the hard chair next to the Formica table. A half dozen takeout containers are strewn across the bed, a gut-busting tour of the bar's menu. The bartender had glanced at her, and at me, then slipped a six-pack in a plastic bag with a wink. As thanks for the order, maybe. Or approval about my choice of company for the night. He asked the guy in the safety vest if he could put it on his tab. Slumped over the bar, the guy gave an unsteady thumbs up. You only live once, he said, the words barely discernible. Carpe-fucking-diem.

"So until now you've always made the run to Winnipeg and back on a single day?"

I nod.

"So that's, what, thirteen, fourteen hours of driving?"

"Longer if the border guys make a show of interrogating every trucker and tourist."

But they can't do it at every crossing. They tried in the days after 9/11, where state troopers and the RCMP right-angled their cruisers across every north-south road, highway or otherwise. A continent too scared to move. Then I get a call from the hospital in Sioux Falls patched through dispatch with few details, a stone-faced Mountie with an assault rifle cradled in his arms, a sympathetic border village without any options to offer a trucker imagining the worst.

"Way too much time behind the wheel for me," she says. "I need my beauty sleep, ha ha. Still, I suppose if you do it enough—"

She carries on. There are more questions, answers. We

talk for a long time, familiar enough not to think too much, a conversation on cruise. Stories about home and life, me growing up in a grimy steeltown out east, my current home in the suburbs stuffy and alien, her life as a lawyer in some eastern city being easy to walk away from. How pills and cash only delay the lawyerly burn and fade. How smart guys end up in trucks pushing goods between cities. How children die, leaving mommies and daddies to stare at unfillable spaces. Then I realize she's stopped talking. Waiting for me to say something.

"I asked if that's crazy," she says.

I tell her of course not, trying to backtrack to whatever point she's defending.

"You just want control of how it all ends," she says. "I'm not depressed—I just don't want to go back to where I've left, you know?"

I'm not sure I believe her. Then she's talking about canyons and bridges and skyscrapers, that there's no plan, that she'll just know. Wondering how far she'll drive before she finds the spot. She wants to fall.

"You don't really want to die," I say.

No response. I hear myself apologizing. I don't know why.

"No, I'm sorry," she says. "For earlier. Don't know why I came on so strong. I walked over through the ash, saw you walk into your room, thought you might like some—"

"Some what?"

"I was going to say comfort, but that's not it. In that moment I felt loose, like I could just take you. Insane, right?"

"No. Well, maybe."

We share a brief laugh.

"Why are you all the way over there?"

Surely it's obvious. Still married, or trying to be. Motel strangers. Complications on a scale I can't fathom.

"Sit beside me," she says.

"I can't."

She sighs.

"There's something here—you can't feel it?"

I focus on breathing. She uncrosses her legs, rises from the floor. A half-step to the chair. Sits in my lap, legs perpendicular to my own, slides an arm around my neck. Lays her cheek against my shoulder. A warmth arrives. Not heat. More like the kindling of some new understanding. Where you know it's all right to stumble in front of each other.

It could be that hours pass like that before she pads to the window and pushes the curtains aside. The ash is almost to the top of the glass. I say my name to her back. She repeats it a few times, testing, before her hand comes up, wiping something away from her face. She comes back to straddle me, mute in this chair, takes my face in her hands. Her lips soft and warm—mine unmoving, words of refusal kept behind. She stretches high to take off her shirt. Lowers her left breast towards me, her nipple a wildberry in my mouth, hard and soft, charcoal and smoke.

It's morning. Yellowed light in the room, bright and late. Patchy. The curtains a dingy plaid. My cellphone buzzes on the nightstand—dispatch, probably, looking for a check-in. I pick up my clothes from the other side of the bed, where the bedspread has been lifted over the other pillow, half-made, smoothed out as I slept. I step around the takeout containers and beercans, my feet making soft prints in the ash just inside the door.

It's blinding outside, and all clear. No ash anywhere out there, not even in the grooves and corners, as though it had never been there at all. The hush of a strong westerly flows around me and back into the room.

I sit in the Muskoka chair and watch the day begin. Fields and trees, landscape flat to the horizon. The motel parking lot is black, recently paved, already warming in the sun. The high fumes of tar and painted lines mix with the smells of wheat and dust. The guy in the orange vest walks out of his room, squints at me, and waves as he climbs into a battered company pickup. He starts the engine, lights a cigarette, and stares through the windshield a long while. Finally, he backs out and eases his way to the mouth of the lot, looking for a break in traffic, southbound, all those vehicles already at highway speed.

QOM

FOR THE FIRST time since he came home, Matt's in bed with me and Sheen. His sleeping chair is empty and cool between the bed and the wall, wedged into perpetual recline. He's on his left side, as close to the edge of the bed as he can be, facing the window above the chair and the drapes that never get fully closed. Hands between his thighs, together, like he's praying. Not sleeping. Me neither.

"A big night," I said right after supper. "Can you—?"

"I'll try."

"Tish said her guy will be here as soon as he can."

"All right."

Parental sleep might come later, a dream we've been cultivating for just over a year. Mine, the mom's dream; Matt's, the dad's. Sheen's out for now, on her back, knees up, hands folded against her chest. Tense. Even her four-year-old sleeping self is waiting for the next episode.

The doctors hate it when we try out different names. Episodes. Attacks. Throes. Just call them seizures, they've said all along. Yesterday, we tried calling them that for the first time, the word in our mouths like steel wool. My sister's call came just as we were getting ready to abandon the word again, go back to the other ones.

"It's just as good as the government shit," she said.

I asked about the ratio.

"He said nine to nine. Said you'd know what that meant."

I could never have imagined the precision. All the information online, cascading down websites in hopeful waterfalls of text. But then there's the consent, the forms, the waiting, the irregular supply. If we had the right doctor, lived in the right city, it'd be easier. But here in Matt's hometown, far north enough that no one offers free shipping, small enough that every diagnostic test requires a drive, the old docs carry some of themselves into their practice. They'd never say they're against the program or the science, but their eyes and shoulders do.

Sheen moans. I get up on an elbow and glance at the clock. Awake, her eyes roll back and she pants for a few moments before the convulsions begin. When she's asleep, they're craftier—she's convulsing almost before I can register the time. Just over an hour since the last one. I wait and worry, make sure the pillow's clear of her contorted face so she won't suffocate, and cry a little every single time. Then it's over—the demons have left her for the swine.

"Daddy?"

"Mommy's right here, baby," I say.

"Daddy!"

That woeful, frustrated tone, wanting to say more. But she's lost months of development along the way, doesn't have many words. It's impossible to quantify, really.

Sheen whimpers and cranes her neck to look at the silk carpet Matt hung there a few years ago. Home on leave, he bragged about bartering with the dealer down to half the asking price. *Nine hundred knots per square inch, pure silk, the Lamborghini of carpets*, he said, proud as a new parent. From Qom, a holy city in Iran. Said the carpets were smuggled into Afghanistan along with the insurgents' weaponry but sold in different markets. A new language of knots, density, weft, warp. Abstract shapes, flowers and spiders and life lines, glowing gently in the jaundiced light slipping in between the drapes. Sheen sighs and her eyes flutter closed, head back onto the pillow, hands together again.

Matt hasn't moved. He says his side of the bed is now hers. That's why he's at the edge—he won't fit in the shape her body's made. Most nights when they can't sleep, he'll turn in his chair and whisper to our daughter the war stories he can't tell me.

At first, the cost seemed such a small concern. Families find a way. The payout from his wounds helped with the mortgage, but not much beyond that. Unlike his Legion buddies, Matt refuses to bitch about it, says it's enough to be out and alive and home. This afternoon, he threw one of those cash-sized envelopes onto the table with a flourish, like it was thicker than it was.

"Broke the bank," Matt said, attempting a joke.

"We shouldn't use our savings," I said, knowing otherwise.

"What's the alternative?"

"Sell blood, maybe?"

"Red Cross doesn't pay."

"Sperm donation?"

"No, that seems like giving too much away."

"A kidney, then."

"What? No—"

He finally saw that I was joking too. Unexpected laughter. A rare current between us. Sudden, wondrous lovemaking against the kitchen counter, Matt sweating through the pain. A breathless, hopeful pause before Sheen moaned from the bedroom again.

There's a soft knock at the front door.

"He's here. You ready?"

"Yes. No. Can you?"

"Sure, babe," I say.

Tish's guy has a shine, like everything he owns is new. Nice but subdued car out front. Thin, precisely trimmed beard, dark eyes. Preppy mall clothes. I expected tracksuits and bling. Expected it to feel more illegal.

"Hi," I say.

"What's your name?"

"Ilona. I'm Sheen's mom."

"All right. May I?"

I step aside and he enters, looking around. Then he's down the hall and into the kitchen and putting small clear packages on the table next to the envelope. Inside each, dusty green buds, woven through with bright orange threads of something.

"Nine to nine," I say. "Right?"

"It's good stuff."

"How's your supply? Is the price stable?"

He gives me a look. "For now. The supply, anyway. The price will go up next time."

"But Tish said—"

He puts up a hand. "This is a long way out, but she told me about the girl, so—"

He pauses, looks away, carrying burdens of his own. "Today it's city price," he finishes. "But it has to go up, you understand?"

I hand over the envelope and he counts the cash. Nods. Gives me a plain card with a number I can call for next time. Tells me not to tell anyone, that we'll be his only customers out here. Says it with weight.

Then he digs into his pocket, pulls out an aluminum tube about the size of a flashlight. "It's a vaporizer. Runs on batteries. No smoke. Weed goes here, draw and inhale up here."

"I don't have any more cash—"

He waves away my words and gets up quickly. "I hope it helps," he says on his way out.

I deadbolt the door behind him, soft as I can.

Another moan from down the hall. I hear Matt speaking to her, low and indistinct. She's always loved his voice, always responds, except in the middle of one. I'd like to believe she can hear him from whichever depths hold her so tightly, but hers is a tough case. There's no cure, none of the medicines work. We gave her street weed every which way but smoking. Matt and I agree about the sensitivity of her lungs and residue getting everywhere. But we were about to do it, if I'm honest, and bought a small pipe. Today's cash was originally for the local guy. Hurt to help, no matter how you look at it.

My hands shake as I open one of the small zippered bags, open the strange device, and pack the chamber.

Turn it on. A pungent smell, stronger than the street stuff. I bring it into the bedroom. Matt's turned, trying to keep her warm against his bare chest. She lies stiffly against him, crying quietly. Something gave during that last one.

"Here," I say, kneeling next to her and wiping my eyes. "Take this and suck on it and then breathe. Or—"

The sudden complexity of how we move oxygen in and out of ourselves overwhelms me. This can't be right—what are we doing to her?

"Wait, sweetie. Stop and we'll—"

Sheen sits up, sniffling, then takes the tube and looks at it a moment. In the dim light I see her seek out his eyes. He nods. She seals the correct end to her mouth. Sucks. Inhales. Deep. Holds all the breath in the room, hers, Matt's, mine. So deep and natural I wonder what magic I'm seeing. Exhales, sinks back onto her pillow, and looks up at the Qom carpet, smiling at the tribal patterns before closing her eyes. She rolls onto her right side, her back against his chest, her breath slowing until, a few moments later, we hear her first soft snores.

When rest is all you have.

Matt looks peaceful, too. Sheen's shielding his entrance wound, a small, jagged star of fading scar tissue just under his ribs. The exit scar on his back is the same colour, just as jagged, triple the size. A razor fragment of shrapnel tore everything up as it passed through. Angry. Sheen gasped when she saw it for the first time. Reached out a clammy, trembling hand, distracted.

"Daddy hurt?"

"Only when I breathe, baby girl."

CUT ROAD

WE STARTED THE fire. Behind us, everything burns. We've made it to the beach and just sit, looking around at the smoke, an omnipresent, choking, swirling god.

"It's crazy, but I still want to get out there and plant," Hezzie says.

Doug, the crew's tree-runner and foreman, sighs. "Me too."

His quad, a red Honda, sits between us and the trail back to camp, idle for the first time in weeks. Gina panicked a few minutes ago and tried to start it up, screaming about getting away. But there's a sequence to it only Doug knows. Hezzie and I made a game of blaming the fire on the machine to calm her. Told her that if the muffler wasn't so damn hot, the leaves and grass in the mud wouldn't have caught fire. A nice distraction, too, from her mania, the awkward aftermath of telling her that I've enjoyed sharing a tent with her over the past weeks, that I had been planning to ask her to move in with me. "Won't happen now, of course," I said. "Ha ha." Not laughing at her, just the situation. She didn't feel the same, obviously.

"You're all institutionalized," I say. "This is like a holiday."

"Screw off," Gina says. "A holiday?"

My eyebrows raise. "*Screw*?"

"Doug doesn't like swearing," she says.

"Actually," he says, "I feel like swearing right now."

"Not praying," I say.

He runs a dirty hand through his shaggy blonde hair, glances back at the treeline. "Nope. Out of material."

"Doug, the hardcore Jesus-whisperer, refusing to pray? Will wonders never cease—"

"Cut it out," Gina says to me. "Doug can believe whatever he wants."

I fold my hands, lift my eyes, and watch the large, dark pieces of ash strolling the heavens as silently as monks. "Dear Lord, help Doug deliver another miracle, like the daily wonders he performs with his almighty Honda ..."

"Amen, brother," Hezzie says. "Amen."

Gina shakes her head, gets up again, and walks away, rubbing her arms, chilled like we all are. The stone beach, littered with driftwood and last-year's dried, faded seaweed, gets into the bones. I watch her go, her filthy cargo pants tucked into her orange caulked boots, tattered old dress shirt hanging on her. If I was poetic, I'd say she was willowy. But even the romantic in me knows she's just skinny, the ideal frame for climbing slash piles to find the perfect spot for the next imperfect tree.

Doug looks at me. "You gonna go after her?"

"She'll be fine. Can't go too far, anyhow. Ha ha."

"Don't be such a jerk. Gina—!" And he's up and

running after her, putting his arm around her thin shoulders, trying to talk her out of walking too far into the haze.

Doug chose the first ten to go. The rescue technician left a satellite radio, said they'd be back for the rest of us. Then the wind changed direction and picked up. By the time the chopper got back, the flames were flashing like yellow lightning through the smoke, the fire roaring and booming and crackling. Overhead, the beating of rotors. The handset crackled, disembodied a voice saying, *Can't land if we can't see—head east towards the lake.* We ran, didn't even grab our packs. Dropped the radio somewhere. Now it's just us, the fire behind, frozen lake in front, the smoke moving over us before diving at the cooler ice a few hundred feet out from shore. We have a little pocket of breathable air, a vaulted cathedral of indistinct grey.

I shiver. Hezzie reaches over and rubs my back. A mostly ineffective gesture, although the brief spots of warmth she moves around with her hand feel nice. Serene. She's in her late thirties, a lifer, dreadlocks woven through with white hairs. Everything she owns seems knitted or sewn together from a hundred other things, like her whole being has been repurposed.

"Want me to light a fire?"

"You're hilarious," I say.

"No, really, I'll just run back in and grab a burning log. Fire's close, won't take long—" She's overcome by coughing, can't finish the joke.

"How about a joint instead?"

She smiles around the coughing attack, eyes red and watering. "I would, sweetie, I really would. But everything's back there."

In the evenings, it was Hezzie, Doug, Gina, and me who lit the campfire. Everyone else went right to bed in daylight, calling us crazy. Here, so far north, the sunset's late, sunrise early. Cold. Three nights ago, Doug rode back to camp late, covered in soot. He knocked smoking mud from the machine. Every trip took twice as long that day because he spent so much time putting out fires. "Only saw the ones I doubled back on," he said. "There have to be more." Despite the late thaw, the forest is dry, even as the snow melts in the trees' shadows. Down south they'd call a fire ban and put park rangers in towers with binoculars. Here, it's just Doug's blue eyes to spot them and his old windbreaker to beat out the flames.

"We have to stay together," he says when he gets back. "If there's a wind shift or a break in the smoke, we have to be ready."

Gina, her head on his shoulder, just nods.

"Haven't heard the rescue chopper in a while," Hezzie says.

We can hear the planes, though, the engines rising and falling as they swoop towards and away from the flames. The rescue guy said the fire we started was Manitoba's biggest so far this year, quoting a number of consumed hectares I can't remember. "Two of the province's three water bombers are here," he said. He seemed so calm. They'd landed the bright yellow helicopter in a clear-cut near camp and shut down the turbines. The crew stayed with the chopper but the two rescue guys walked over to the camp, impossibly bright in their blaze orange jump-suits. Drank our coffee. Eyed the women.

Doug and Gina sit, their shoulders touching. A hot,

fire-fed gust of wind rushes through the trees and past us, rippling the surface of the open water between beach and ice. We all jump at a booming sound.

"Fuck, that was close," I say.

"Must have been the Nodwell," Doug says.

Gina looks at her watch. "So soon?"

I wonder out loud why we didn't hear the camp's propane tanks go first. Doug doesn't respond, just stares at the grey beach stones. Gina's hand creeps out and rubs his forearm.

The company flew him in a week early to set up. Kitchen tent, cook shack, showers, generator, water pump. He smiled the most—being a church guy, he's always smiling—when he talked about digging the latrine I called the Shit Pit. "It was a blessing to have it ready for you guys." The rest of us were supposed to come in by longboat from the settlement at the southern end of the lake, but ice-out was late. Instead, we piled ourselves and our gear onto the rusty old Nodwell and churned hours away along old logging roads mostly reclaimed by muskeg. That machine broke down the first week, the generator about a week ago. *We can still finish this*, we said, laughing at cold showers and the dark. We walked everywhere, each day a little longer as we planted clear-cuts farther and farther from camp. Doug had confidence they'd bring out the parts in time.

"Now we'll have to walk out," Hezzie says, and starts coughing again.

No one laughs. Before he became just another tree planter waiting on a cold, cut off beach, Doug's final act as foreman was to quad out along the cut roads as far as he dared. The fire pushed him back to us. "It's everywhere," he said as he parked his machine, leaving the key in the ignition, which he never does.

"Or swim," Gina says. "Out to the ice."

She's serious, but there's no point in saying anything. Too far, too deep, too cold.

We jump again at a series of loud cracks, followed by crashes and groans, an upswell in the nearing roar I'd almost convinced myself I couldn't hear any longer. A hungry fire will leap between trees like an acrobat and sweep along the ground faster than its own wind. So loud, so fast. Gina tries to pull away when I reach out and take her hand.

"Don't," she yells.

"But I love you!"

I think I hear Doug telling me to leave her alone, his low voice a whisper against the storm. The first hot embers begin to float past, black sprites fringed in yellows, oranges, reds. Beautiful, hopeless chemistry. None seem to land anywhere. Not on the beach, the four of us, the water, the ice so far from shore.

BAYFRONT

THEY HAD REMOVED the handcuffs but hadn't let Willem have his Bible during trial, he told her. Nor did he have to swear on one, much to his disappointment, just hold up a hand and promise to say the right things. He sat in that bulletproof witness box, hands free but empty, watching the members of the court move testimony and evidence around like they were shuffling cards. For some reason, though, he loved the memory of the hard bench in the defendant's box. Beneath him, it had warmed quickly. Lacquered red oak, its grain a dark topography.

Sanaz loved that detail. "Like you were sitting on one of your pews," she said.

"Seems like a long time ago," he said.

"This is ironic, right?"

"Yes."

Cloudy skies. The water flagstone grey. The October wind across the bay had died down. It had been strong enough to push Willem's hair straight back like the fins of an old Cadillac, but now it just lifted a few at a time. Caught wisps of Sanaz's black hair that had escaped her hijab, too. A loose bit of metal near the head of a mast in the marina banging an alarming tattoo had fallen silent.

He didn't know why today was the day to tell her the most uncomfortable portion of his story. They'd been meeting for months on this bayside bench, his favourite place, their initial small talk shifting to her needs, with him falling easily back into old pastoral ways, mostly listening. There were immigration and family concerns. Distant relatives in Iran seeking sponsorship. An ex-husband who from time to time still showed up at the bayside café where she made fancy drinks and cut sandwiches, demanding she come home to their arranged marriage. A new life unable to carve away an old one.

"Much of the story I knew," she said. "But the newspapers were certain you were guilty."

His eyebrows lifted. "How—?"

"I searched on the internet, of course," she said, patting the charcoal sleeve of his blazer with a patient hand.

"Oh, yes. Right."

"Even afterwards, it was like they could not let go," she said.

"I know."

"This is why you left the church."

"Trust is hard to repair."

Her hand remained on his arm for a long moment as she watched the waves. She had such long fingers, delicate enough to pluck single strands from a spiderweb without disturbing any of the others. Remarkable hands. Decorated by henna that had faded to a distant orange, its intricate swirls and loops and flowers becoming indistinct, more stain than art. Too bad, really. It was gorgeous work, applied by a friend to mark the first anniversary of leaving her husband. Because of an ultraconservative father and a wilting mother, it was only the second time she had ever had it done. Her wedding, at eighteen, the first.

She withdrew her hand at the sound of purposeful steps on the asphalt behind them. Willem glanced down, a quick check of the distance between them, instinctual propriety. She was a practicing Muslim, after all. He asked her once why she still chose to wear the hijab. *It's not required*, she said, *but it keeps Muslim men from hissing at me on the street.* He hadn't known that this was a reality away from Iran. *Muslim men are Muslim men everywhere.*

"Hello, Father."

A tall security officer in a neon yellow windbreaker stood next to them. Robotic wraparound sunglasses with yellow lenses. A long, black Mag-Lite dangling from a metal loop on his utility belt. Tan lines on his brow and neck fading with the autumn weather. Cleanly shaved. Creases. He'd wanted to be a cop, Willem imagined, a youth spent looking towards a career in law enforcement, a failed test or physical ailment sending him to security work instead. A poor substitute yet a kind of refusal to give in.

"How long will I have to ask you to stop calling me Father?"

"Soon as you stop wearing the collar."

Willem shifted on the bench and shook his head.

Sanaz turned. "Why would you call him that? He is not Catholic."

"He knows that," Willem said.

"And you are—"

"Sanaz. A friend. And you?"

"Special Officer Heddon, ma'am. Do you know who he really is?"

"Yes. I do."

Heddon looked at her through his jaundiced lenses a long moment, his face neutral. Willem watched him make a quick scan of her from her head to her feet, resting on the flour and spattered milk on her black work shoes. He nodded, returning his gaze to the grey water a few hundred feet offshore.

"Calm now," he said.

A few days later, Sanaz asked to walk along the waterfront rather than sit on the bench. There was a gaggle of labourers on the pier setting up for a weekend festival of some kind. Games. Rides for the kids. Funnel-cakes and deep-fried chocolate bars. With vehicles and activity blocking their way, Willem and Sanaz walked in the other direction, strolling instead through the marina and along the paved paths in Bayfront Park. The weather forecast had been wrong, the sun burning through the predicted cold rain like it had something to prove. Thunderstorms and fierce winds the day before had scrubbed the park clean, the paths and grassy areas clear apart from beneath a few stubborn trees that finally relinquished their last leaves to the fall.

"Why do you still wear the collar?"

"I'm surprised it's taken you this long to ask," Willem said.

"That police officer the other day—"

"Security officer. Heddon."

"—he thinks you are guilty. Why?"

"I'm not sure. Maybe he has some connection to Bethany."

"Bethany?"

"The girl."

"Ah. The newspapers did not name her."

"No, they wouldn't," he said.

"So you do not know him?"

"No. I mean, yes, I know him now."

"He bothers you often?"

"Almost every day. But I'm not bothered—he needs someone to watch, that's all."

"He is very hostile."

Willem laughed quietly. "Maybe," he said. "But he still stops."

"Like me."

"Like you."

"You wear the collar for us, then."

"No."

"For yourself?"

He shook his head.

"Allah?"

"For God," he said. "Yes, I suppose that's it."

Sanaz smiled, bright against her navy blue hijab and black café shirt peeking out from her jacket collar. Willem was glad for the lightness, a rare thing. Too many cares had been applied to her face in the form of pimples and patches of dry skin.

"I think you are not trying to convert me," she said.

"Should I be?"

"Of course!"

"What I mostly do is run away. I'm not a very good missionary."

"But you sit still on that bench for me every day."

"I do."

"A strange kind of—of—"

"Ministry."

"That is the word, yes."

"Young lady, you'll get no argument from me on that score."

The park was quiet, with only the bravest runners and cyclists defying the anticipated forecast. Four or five degrees warmer than expected, the sun adding depth to the warmth in the air. They flashed past with serious, determined expressions, peeling off layers and unzipping jackets. Wrapping, tying, stuffing them wherever they could find space. You could go for hours with such preparation, he thought. Self-contained.

A few minutes later, he asked, "So why are we walking?"

"From inside the café, I saw the sun come out. Not many days like this left."

"True."

"I wonder if you will be as brave when the snow falls. To meet me, I mean."

Willem didn't respond. He had many questions for her, ones that would lead her to explain about this departure from their routine. But he felt that she should speak first. He reached out and pulled a few faded, desiccated berries from a pathside bush. Then he felt foolish for taking them as well as for keeping them in his hand. When she looked away from the water, up towards the city, he dropped them to the side of the path, where they bounced and rolled and made irregular escapes into the weeds.

"Somehow Abdullah got my new mobile number, and has been calling a lot. Calling the café, too. Somehow he knows about you. He thinks—" A pause. "He thinks that we are together. I have tried to explain, but it is difficult without bringing religion into it."

"He's upset that you're speaking to an old, fallen Reverend?"

"No, that I am speaking to a Christian man at all."

"You can reassure him that I'm no—"

"You are. He has threatened you."

"So you're getting me away from the bench."

"Yes."

"Thank you, Sanaz. But you don't have to do that. I'm a good runner, remember?"

"You are a good man."

I'm not, he thought. But it was nice that she thought so.

Sanaz pulled out her phone, a shiny thing that looked made entirely of glass, and stared a long moment at the screen. Willem frowned at the presumption, that whatever she'd found was more important than just walking and talking with him. She apologized and said that she had taken out the phone just to see the time, but a text message from Abdullah had distracted her. She laughed when he asked how it was possible to see the time, and gently turned them around so she wouldn't be late back to work.

"You need a phone," she said.

"Who would I call?"

"I'd feel better."

"It would just sit in my pocket like a stone. If I remembered to take it with me at all."

"I could call you."

"You know where to find me."

"But you always wait for me."

When they arrived back to the café, there were more workers on site, cursing and yelling at the booths and rides they were assembling. An enormous groaning sound stretched along the pier, followed by shouts of alarm. One of the vertical supports for a kiddie ride was falling in slow motion, the metal lattice twisting, as though someone had forgotten to fully wrench the bolts at ground level. When it reached the ground, the sound was a subdued clang, the upright not falling with enough speed to be any louder. The workers gathered around the fallen steel and made emphatic hand gestures.

"No one thinks about safety anymore," he said. "Someone could get killed."

❧

When Sanaz arrived at the bench the next day, Friday, she looked pleased with herself. Her face was at peace and relaxed, her blemishes calm. Willem enjoyed the idea that she looked forward to their lunchtime meetings as much as he did. Maybe I'm good for her skin, he thought. As she arranged herself and her lunch, balancing the bags and leftover containers on the wooden slats engraved with years of use and the initials of a dozen young lovers, she talked a bit about her day and how busy the café was, despite the weather. She brought a blanket, too, thick fleece the colour of windswept lake ice, and arranged it around her legs. And a bag, bright red, with a box inside.

"Open it," she said.

The box contained a new mobile phone. Small, black as charcoal. A simpler model than her touchscreen wonder, but still a thousand times more complex than he could imagine needing. He pulled out a sheaf of printed papers slid in beside the box. She pointed at the bottom of the final page.

She said, "It is your new number. And the phone number to call when you need to top up your minutes."

"I have no idea what that means."

"You will. Just read the papers."

"Thank you."

"It is nothing. Just a prepaid phone. Cheap."

"Can I—"

"No. My gift to you."

He returned the phone to its box and put everything back in the bag. He would have repaid her had she hesitated in any way, but it was oddly comforting that he didn't have to. It seemed to fit, this thing she'd done for him, although he couldn't explain why. He'd never enjoyed gifts—he never knew how to respond.

Before everything fell, small gifts would occasionally appear in the parsonage's mailbox. Presents for the flock's watchful shepherd. The notes were usually unsigned, though he'd often match the handwriting against offering envelopes and other paperwork. Some were signed, of course, like the one from Bethany who eventually cried her way into charges against him. He should have given it right back. Her accusations were a public shock yet everyone assumed he was guilty. A quick trial, in the end, due to insufficient evidence. Her family offering an indifferent apology to please the church elders. Saving face. Still, you can't fix shattered glass. You wonder if you might have supplied the rock that went through. Looked a little too long. Touched an arm or shoulder at a wrong moment. Smiled a little too often. Accepted the wrong gift.

"You should keep it out," Sanaz said. "I can help you practice."

"Let me look it over tonight. Tomorrow?"

"Tomorrow. Promise?"

A low laugh. "Promise."

One of the festival workers jumped away from the crowd-control fence he was assembling and swore at top volume. He sucked on a knuckle while his coworkers laughed. He gave them all the finger before replacing the glove and leaning back into his task. The festival was nearly assembled for tomorrow's opening. The workers had been practice-running the rides when Willem had arrived and the Ferris wheel was still running, faux-organ music sounding distorted against its own echoes. Willem and Sanaz watched it turn against the sky. The motion was deceptively lulling and Willem lost himself for a few moments, coming to only to realize Sanaz had begun speaking to him.

"I'm sorry?"

"I was just saying that I would not have sat down if you had not been wearing the collar," she said.

He grunted. "It can be rather disarming."

"I had seen you a few times."

"I didn't know that. Why did you wait?"

"The bench seemed like it was yours."

His face tensed and he exhaled. "More Neil's than mine."

Sanaz watched him closely but didn't speak. Leaving space for him to fill. There was always the question of how much to say, how much of himself to tear open. Neil, the only kid from the youth group to stay in contact after the trial. Neil, the star everything: youth leader, student, athlete, activist. Neil asking Willem for a character reference on his eighteenth birthday so he could enlist in the army and disappoint everyone who had higher hopes for him. Neil soaring through training, a leader in the making. Neil riding shotgun when the IED obliterated his vehicle.

"He was in the youth group at my church," Willem said. "He always had a lot of questions, so we'd meet here. He died a couple years ago. Afghanistan."

"Oh, my God—I am so sorry."

For a long moment, he looked at the festival chaos. "Me, too."

On the bench between them, Sanaz's phone began buzzing. She picked it up, glanced at the screen, and frowned. She returned it to its place, face down against the worn, faded wood, and looked out at the harbour where a late-season sailboat nudged through the waves, its white sail waving with and against the wind.

At first, Sanaz's text messages came quickly to his new device, one after the other, as though he was being goaded into a response. Brief previews lit up his screen, momentary, before his new device went dark again. He didn't know how to retrieve them. By the end of the second day, the messages had slowed. Not judgment, exactly, but more of a given space that seemed to say, *You come to me.*

He hadn't read the material that came with the phone. On Friday afternoon, he'd been driven from the harbourfront earlier than usual by the frantic sounds from the crew setting up the festival. It was to open that evening, so last-minute preparations were at full pace, tempers flaring. And then his foot slipped on a bit of carrot rind on his apartment stairs while he was taking out the recycling, twisting something in his right knee. By Saturday morning, the pain was enough to send him to a walk-in clinic, where the tired doctor pressed and prodded and said it was soft-tissue damage. *That's why you're in so much pain*, he said. *Sprains usually hurt more than fractures.* Willem was prescribed a codeine painkiller and the rest of the day slipped away. Laid up in his flat with his leg elevated, he'd resolved to get down to the bayfront on Sunday. He had a plan. Dig out the old walking stick and be on the bench in time for Sanaz's lunch break. Maybe she'd give him a tutorial about his new phone.

When he arrived, he checked his watch as he eased himself down onto the bench. A few minutes late. Sanaz nowhere in sight. Maybe the weather finally kept her away. A damp, cold wind clipped across the bay, lifting the tops of the whitecaps away. The booths and game tents billowed wetly with each gust, and a grating howl cut through the stationary structure of the mini-Ferris-wheel. A few brave families and fun-seekers milled around the festival with the hollow look you get when you're beaten by the wind for too long. He buttoned his old beige trench coat to his throat and dug his hands into his pockets.

Heddon stood with a few of his security colleagues at the entrance, a break in the crowd-control fencing, looking miserable in their standard-issue neon windbreakers and black cargo-style uniforms that seemed to do little against the elements. He was the only one not smoking, standing slightly away, as though he wanted to avoid breathing in their second-hand insubordination. Willem sighed when Heddon sauntered over.

"Got stood up, Father?"

"Do we have to do this now?"

"Cute thing like her finally wised up, eh?"

The comment was grit in Willem's eye. He looked up, about make a sharp remark about Heddon's status as a *Special* Officer of the security variety, when he saw the dark smudges under Heddon's eyes. His words, too, had been delivered with half their normal intensity. Rote, almost. No, Willem thought, the man is exhausted. Cutting deeper risked too much of the underlying tissue.

"Must be the weather," Willem said. "She's always here."

"What else could it be, right?"

"Right."

"Couldn't be an old man sitting too close to the wrong girl. Again."

"Look, I—"

"There's no loitering on the waterfront."

"Hold on—"

"You'll have to move on."

"No."

"What did you say?"

"I said no. I'm not doing anything wrong."

Heddon took a step closer, moving his hands towards his utility belt. Obviously to intimidate, but it looked more like he was trying to hike up his pants. Willem was horrified to discover laughter trying to escape through his teeth. He bit it back and raised his hands, palms forward, the most disarming gesture he could think of. A barrier of loose skin, bones, tendons, age spots, silver hairs. He heard placating words coming out of his own mouth, strangely calm, acquiescing to Heddon's demand. The greater risk being laughter thrown in the security officer's face.

But Heddon had stopped listening, looking past Willem to some point down the asphalt pier. Willem followed the look. A tall man in a puffy black coat was watching them, the wind buffeting his loose athletic pants. A thick beard. Darker skin than Willem's but still pale in the cold air.

"Friend of yours?"

"No," Willem said. "I've never seen him."

"The coat's too thick. It's not that cold."

As Heddon reached for the radio handset clipped to the front of his jacket, the man turned and walked away. They watched him go, Heddon's hand letting go of the radio and falling to his side. He muttered something unintelligible.

"I'm sorry?"

"Too much paperwork," Heddon said. "Easier if he just leaves."

A muffled tune came from somewhere nearby. Heddon nodded at Willem's coat pocket.

"Your phone's ringing, Father."

But by the time he retrieved it from the inside breast pocket, the noise had stopped. The screen was still lit, blue fire against the day's gloom, an unfamiliar number on the screen. It was probably Sanaz, calling about her no-show, but he had no idea how to return the call. Maybe she couldn't get away from work. He got up and started to walk towards the café. The bad knee buckled. Bright pain and nausea as he sank back onto the bench.

"Jesus," Heddon said. "You look like death."

"Hurt my knee."

"Do I have to call an ambulance for you now?"

"No, I have some pills."

Heddon pulled out an unopened bottle of water from a large pocket on his uniform pants. Held it out without comment.

"Thank you," Willem said.

As Willem cracked the bottle's seal, the security guard shrugged and walked away, back towards the break in the fencing.

The next morning, a single white trailer marked with the initials of a distant amusement company, all that remained of the festival, sat in the far corner of the parking lot like a forgotten toy. Greasy food containers and other unidentifiable garbage blew around the grounds in compact, ankle-nipping twisters.

When he walked into the café, only a few tables were occupied. The barista, a young woman maybe a week out of her teens, stared off into space and wiped the same small circle on the counter with a grimy cloth. She glanced at his clerical collar when he spoke, falling into the stuttering discomfort young people often felt around him.

"I, um—who?"

"Sanaz. She works here. Is she in today?"

"Oh, her. No, they called me in to cover."

"Will she be in later?"

"Who knows? She was a no-show yesterday, too."

"We were supposed to meet yesterday."

She shrugged. "Claire said she saw her come in to get her things, said she looked mad. Or sad. Or scared. I forget which."

"Claire?"

"One of the girls. Can I get you something?"

"No, thanks. Can you pass along a message—"

"Don't you have her number?"

Willem pulled out the new phone.

"I don't," he said. "Well, I guess I might, but ... Do you?"

"No. The manager will, though."

"May I speak with him?"

"Her, actually. But—"

She tilted her head and gave him a look.

"Ah, right," he said. Privacy concerns. "Of course not."

"Right."

He still had the little phone in his hand when he left. The café had been constructed on a jetty that protruded like a finger into the bay, surrounded on three sides by water. He walked out the side entrance and moved to the water's edge, leaning on the guardrails set up there.

He made his way slowly along the water, leaning on the walking stick a little more, allowing the injury to bloom rather than upping his painkillers. The weather was mild and the sun shone on the shoulders of his trench coat as though willing him, like in that old fable, to take it off. But he didn't; it was still too cool to move around in just a dress shirt. The air, as usual, was quick, raising the chop on the bay and unsettling the few late-season yachts still tied up in the marina.

The rising sound of a police siren echoed around the inlet and off the café walls. One second it sounded as though it was coming from the city, and the next, the park. Finally, with a rush and a roar, a police boat sped through the gap in the marina breakwater, chirping its siren once, twice, before slowing and heaving-to just off the farthest set of jetties. Willem raised his hand against the sun, unable to discern anything more than the police boat, some white-suited figures, and a couple of police vehicles idling on shore. All with lights flashing, the blue, red, red, blue of emergency strobes.

As he moved closer, he saw that another police boat was already there, a semirigid skiff with a pair of wetsuited divers peering into the water below. Two dark heads broke the surface, lenses glinting in the sunlight. A long, white object was floated to the boat and brought onboard. The divers were helped onboard also, and the boat nosed into the dock. As the white object was lifted and handed to a crew of white-suited technicians, a bare, pale foot, unmistakably female, popped free from the wrapping. A body. A female's body.

"No," he said. "Please, Jesus, no."

He limped over to the marina entrance as fast as his bad knee allowed, but the entire marina was closed, cordoned off by obscenely bright police tape. He lifted and stepped under a strand. There was a loud curse, the sound of a cardboard cup being dropped to the ground, and the shuffling of feet. A flash of neon yellow entering his field of vision from the right. A hand on his arm. Firm.

"Father, stop," Heddon said. "You can't go in there."

"Let me through."

"You're not allowed. The police—"

"I saw a body."

"No, you didn't. It's—"

"She didn't come, yesterday or today. It might be her."

Before Heddon could speak, his colleague, who hadn't come over to help, laughed out loud. A sniggering, mocking laugh. Heddon gave him a look, and the laughter quieted.

"They're just dummies," Heddon said.

"What do you mean?"

"The divers and techs are just practicing. The dummies get weighted and thrown into the water so they can bring them back up."

"So there's no—"

"Do you think I'd be allowed to be here if it was real? I'm no cop."

"I guess not, but—"

"Get him out of here," the other officer said. "We'll get our asses fired."

"You have to go."

Willem felt a confusing rush of relief and worry moving from his core and up his throat, pulling at each other and forcing him to gag. The world seemed narrower, somehow.

"I feel sick," he said. "I need to sit down."

Heddon grabbed an arm and led him to a nearby palette of new lumber, helped him sit, and waited nearby. The wood was angular, sun-warmed, and smelled of sap and sawdust. Willem took his phone out again and began pushing buttons, moving through its dizzying array of icons and commands. He recognized nothing, his vision becoming blurred, the sounds around him hollow. Heddon tried to talk him through the simplicities of calling and texting, menus and inboxes, pushing the little green button, how easy it all was. The words had zero meaning. Heddon took the phone and pushed a button, held it to his ears, waited.

"No one's answering," he said.

Willem heard himself talking about Sanaz and danger and needing to make sure that she was all right, about calling back and leaving messages and needing patience and more time. It came out in a jumbled rush, gibberish even to his own ears. Heddon squirmed as Willem tried again and again. Eventually, any grace in the air dissolved. The phone was shoved back into his pocket and the cane returned to his grasp. There were rough hands on his arms leading him away and a familiar voice, hard, telling him to go back to his bench on the waterfront.

A WEEK ON THE WATER

A **FEW WEEKS** ago, I asked to work days but the manager just smirked. I told him it was a bitch to get buses up the escarpment late at night and that sleeping through the day made it hard to see my son. He balled up my Kelly green apron and flung it against my chest. I almost dropped it, its ties cascading from my hands halfway to the floor like entrails. "Guess you shouldn't have fucked up so bad, then," he said.

All you can do is ask, I think, waiting for the tip of my fishing rod to dance.

I don't argue anymore. It's a hard habit to break but that former edge, the strongest and most successful part of myself, won't help me. Better for it to sit in my stomach like a river stone—one of the native guys inside said that if you swallow enough of them the appetite goes away. He didn't seem like he was particularly plugged in to the spirit side of things and was probably making things up as he went—like all of us—but I guess the idea works just fine, apart from wondering where the stones will end up.

"Greenie still giving you grief?"

Gram's cigarette dances on his lower lip with every

syllable. I met him almost a week ago. He's out fishing every day too.

"Always," I say.

"That whole place is green," he said on Tuesday. I had just told him about the supermarket where I worked nights and he went straight to the colour scheme. I didn't say much, but I told him about the manager who makes me sign my paycheque over to him every two weeks then pays me in cash, significantly reduced. "After taxes," he always says with a sneer. Yesterday, Gram decided to call him Greenie.

He spits. "God, I hate that part of the city. Did I tell you I used to have a house up there, right across the street from all those big box stores?"

"No," I say.

He smiles. His teeth used to be perfect, I can see.

"Yeah, paid for that bad boy in cash. All those fat, bored housewives looking for a little something. Suburban junkies—best market ever."

"You don't live up there anymore."

A dark look deepens his features, fleeting, and he gives a lipless smile. But he doesn't reply. You learn not to ask when they're not offering, so I take a small piece of chicken liver and thread it onto the treble hook.

We're on the harbour side of the fishway, next to the recreation path, dropping for catfish. The secret is the bait; it has to be smelly and full of proteins so the cats can find it. Gram's working some old Fancy Feast cat food in surgical tubing and he's had better luck. He said I could try some of his, but my grandfather swore by liver and I'm stubborn about these things. Still, I haven't caught a thing, a week of lob cast after lob cast and waiting while the current dilutes the juices in the meat before having to do it all over again. There's something about loyalty, though.

I don't mind the job, despite my douchebag boss. The store's open twenty-four hours a day but most of the restocking happens overnight, when there are fewer customers to get in the way. They have to pay a night manager, a cashier, and a small army of guys who need to work at night: even though they only open one checkout and dim the lights in the storeroom I can't imagine how they make any money. Not my call—in my former life I'd have cringed at the business model, unknowing that one moment of weakness and seven long years would erase the need to worry about anything greater than working a night shift, getting to bed afterwards, and channel fishing as daily therapy.

Gram's rig dips and drifts. He picks it up from the little rack he's spiked into the ground and holds it away from himself, eyes closed, feeling the bite. A quick upward pull to set the hook and the fish, feeling the tug, tries to run towards the harbour. It's all over in less than a minute. Such a narrow channel and there's nowhere to go, and the fish can't fathom the disparity in physics between the rod and reel and its own finite strength. It's a good one, three or four pounds, and Gram lifts it out of the water with a thumb in its gaping mouth. A thin line of bright red blood runs down its grey belly and drips steadily onto the gravel shoreline. The fish gives a weak twitch of its tail, flinging blood all over.

"Ah, shit, I hate it when they bleed," he says, holding the cat away from his body and wiping the hem of his rain jacket.

"He'll bleed out, I think."

"Yeah, we hooked the gills."

Using the treble hook is a conscious choice. Cats almost always swallow the small trebles whole and the points work hell on their insides. Some guys bend and break off the barbs at each razor point but we don't, preferring a good hook set to the more sporting approach of catch-and-release. Gram likes the taste of catfish but admits that he's too lazy to take them home and clean them. I'd do it, but the halfway house frowns on the mess and smell of gutting and frying the catch. If they live, we toss them back into the channel; if they don't, we leave them out for the birds and animals to take care of. But it's been a cold few days, so maybe the animals can't smell the ones Gram gill-hooked and left to die pale, bloodless deaths.

We still have the conversation we've had all week, though.

"You gonna do something with this one?"

"Can't," he says.

"Me neither."

On Wednesday, I learned that Gram changed his name after he dropped out from college to deal full time ("I used to be a Graham," he said laughing. "Get it?"). It was a really slow fishing day, kind of windy and choppy on the harbour side, so we set up on the marsh side next to the fishway. They set up a barrier across the Desjardins Canal to act like a sieve, keeping the mature carp, big suckers who feed on the bottom, from swimming in and upsetting the plant life. Hard to believe one species can ruin so much water. I don't think either of us got even a nibble from the native marsh fish. Gram did most of the talking that day. Most days, actually—not arguing so much anymore leaves a lot less for me to say.

Gram pulls out a joint the size of my pinkie and asks if I want to spark up. I shake my head, conscious of the weekend cyclists and rollerbladers hissing past.

"Relax, man, we're too far down the trail."

He giggles—a grating sound in the cool air—and tries to light it. It's calm today, the birds making perfect mirror images of themselves on the channel, but damp too, so the J won't stay lit. After a few tries he swears, the scorched tip bouncing like the head of an impatient, greasy maggot.

Then it's the tip of my rod bowing towards the algae-green water and I'm up trying to set the hook. But it pulls too easy. I missed the hit, figure the cat must've nabbed the liver and spit it out before I could hook him. I reel it in, the bright sinker emerging from the underwater gloom followed by the leader and treble. Bare, as though the fish's tongue was able to weave itself around and through the barbs gently enough to take the bait but not get caught.

"Took my bait," I say as I pinch and skewer another bit of bloody liver.

Gram doesn't say anything. Unusual. Just before I lob out my rig, I look over at him. He's zoned right out, staring at the far bank, through the ground, maybe, or into the past he talks about so much I wonder if he's lying. Just to have a story. I knew guys like that inside, so wrecked they'd talk and talk even after getting beaten up for saying the wrong thing. There was this one guy who walked up to the new ones at intake and told each of them a different story about how he ended up there. One day I watched him get his head caved in by a skinhead who probably wasn't even listening but needed to hurt someone anyhow.

I wave my hand in front of his face. Nothing.

"Don't bother when he gets like that—too much of his own product for too long," a voice says from behind.

A pair of bike cops, top-heavy in body armour and utility belts and bright yellow jackets, have ridden up without a sound and stopped at the edge of the paved path behind us. Spindly legs, ridiculous black socks and safety shoes, wraparound sunglasses. I almost laugh but the J is still hanging from Gram's mouth, and the one who spoke, the bigger one, looks like the type to get worked up over a single joint.

"Isn't that right, Gram?"

Gram blinks a few times and turns towards the cops. He gives a dopey smile, looks past the big one, and tilts his head in a hopeful greeting towards the other guy.

"Hey, Wharton."

"Gram."

Wharton, the smaller one who's as pale as our dead fish on the shoreline, says this without taking his eyes from the water on the other side of the fishway. He leans across the handlebars of his police-issue mountain bike and simply studies Cootes Paradise like he's thinking about taking his next holiday there. Gram slips the J into his pocket, but neither of the cops says anything about that. He fidgets. A tight soundtrack of spare change and hidden keys. The big guy nods at me and asks me my name.

The new me grits his teeth and tells him.

"Holy fuck! Almost a week of fishing and I never even knew his name!"

Gram's too excited, hoping this new interesting tidbit will distract everyone, maybe. The big cop dismounts, clicks down the kickstand and steps unevenly across the stones to the edge of the water. Turns towards me, takes off his glasses, and scratches a patch of missed stubble with a fingernail. The arms of his Oakleys swing and knock against his chin with each scratch.

"Anything biting?"

"Not today, no."

Now that he's closer he looks even bigger. His expensive sunglasses have stencilled tan lines on his cheekbones. I don't have to ask to know there are equally sharp lines on his thick biceps and thighs and calves; a creature of routine, every item of uniform put on the same way every time. He doesn't look like the type of guy to be a bike cop—he'd look more at home squeezed behind the steering wheel of one of those smaller new cruisers and harassing kids on skateboards.

"We heard you were out," he says. "Shame they couldn't put you somewhere else."

Wharton is ignoring the waves of cliché his partner is putting out. He's closed his eyes and turned his face towards the muddy sun trying to peek through the clouds. Gram fidgets next to me, a sparrow trying not to get noticed as it hops between tables looking for crumbs. I don't say anything, just dangle the liver-baited rig over the water and lob it out. It sinks without a ripple. I sit back down onto my blue Igloo cooler.

"Are we going to have any trouble with you?"

I shake my head, taking exactly one second for each side to keep the redness from blinding me.

"No, sir."

"No, sir," Gram parrots.

As the big one nods and starts back to his bike, Wharton begins to speak, never opening his eyes or turning his face away from the warmth he's found, and suddenly I know which of these two I'm really going to have to worry about.

"See, that's the thing about the big ones—trafficking, rape, homicide—what actually happens looks so different after the courts get done with it."

Two of those were meant for me. Gram took the other in with a little whimper, his brag and bluster dissolved like sugar in hot water.

"And it concerns me to find you here, close enough to the home you've been ordered to stay away from that it's obvious you're not ready to move on, but far enough away that you could honestly say it's about the fishing."

Gram's shoulders relax and he studies the place where his line disappears into the water. I can almost hear him clueing in that the cops aren't really concerned about him at all.

"Your record says you're smart. Clever too, maybe. But then, I was never a fan of clever," Wharton says.

I don't argue anymore, I want to say.

Wharton opens his eyes and takes another long look at the calm water on the other side of the fishway, waiting for his partner to mount his bike. Then the cops pedal slowly away, nodding and smiling at the pedestrians and other cyclists on the harbour side of the path, ringing their handlebar bells for the kids. Gram fishes quietly beside me having decided, I know, to wait until later to Google his new fishing friend. I probably won't see him tomorrow, Sunday, my last day of work and fishing before my Monday off. I'll go back to hooking channel cats on my own and watching the path, hoping someone in that home will decide that it's a nice enough day for a walk, maybe, down by the marsh.

PIECES OF ECHO

NOT TEN MINUTES after we arrive at the camel racing club, Edie says the second wrong thing. She's already in the wrong section, the men's VIP viewing lounge, and surrounded by blinding tiers of Kuwaitis in white dishdashas. She insisted. I was hoping she'd behave.

"Of course the oil will run out," she says. "It's simple math."

Dhari gives me a look. "You should control your woman, Daniel."

I cringe but say nothing. I don't know who to defend. She refuses to check her words even in delicate situations, a persona she's been developing since we arrived in Kuwait a few months ago, hired by an international school to teach wealthy Arab kids. I know it's just painted on, and there are worse places to be the say-anything-go-any-where-I-want woman, but these oil-rich men in their impossibly clean outfits are our hosts.

The race begins with a crackle of noise from the PA system, drowning out my attempt to rebuke her. Quick decision, in the end. Dhari is the emir's grandson, and he lets me drive his biggest, fastest, most expensive toys.

Edie is always pushing, pushing, even at home, so I go out a lot. "No man should smoke alone," Dhari said the day he discovered me wreathed in grape-flavoured shisha smoke in a neighbourhood café. He was slumming it away from his palace, trying to blend in, and used me as camouflage. We met up again the next week, and the one after that, and soon enough it was every other day. Shisha became Ferraris and Bentleys, ridiculously ornate meals, expeditions on yachts, racing boats that move faster than thought. He supplies Edie and me with the bacon and booze that's supposed to go to the embassies but sits in a government warehouse instead. We went falconing once, the raptors tracking back to the camel-hide gauntlet with prizes of raw rodent meat.

The camels raise a plume of dust, obscuring the desert behind them, and lope around the final curve towards the finish line. Robot jockeys, remote-controlled, boy-sized contraptions, whip their reins across the hides of the yawning beasts. A herd of SUVs runs just behind, drivers and controllers invisible behind tinted glass. Dhari eases his bulk from the leather viewing chair and yells at his camel, his jowls quivering. I can't tell which animal to cheer for. "You must come—these are special races," he said a few days ago, dismissing my weak refusal. I'd already been to the camel racing club on a trip arranged for the new teaching staff. Edie stayed at home that time with a headache from all the dust in the air. In the city we get dust storms. Out here they're sandstorms, clouds of tiny pieces of shell and gritty debris that will scour the skin from your face.

She's forgotten about politics and is cheering like the

men. Up from her seat, yelling at one of the anonymous animals to get a move on, that all her dinars are riding on it, that Baby needs a new pair of shoes. That one gets me, and I rub something from my eye. The men are distracted from the race by her antics so when the first camel crosses the line, she's the only one yelling.

"Edie, take it down a notch," I say.

"Dan, did you see it? My guy passed everyone. We fucking won!"

Like it was a big payday, even though none of our money ever touched the track. I look at Dhari and give an apologetic shrug. He makes a sucking noise behind his teeth.

"This is not how a woman should behave," he says.

She asks, "Are there any more races? Can we bet on the next one?"

Dhari shifts, looking at her with renewed interest, as though he passed by a tarnished coin earlier and has come back to find it polished.

"You would like to wager?"

"Shit, yeah," she says. "This is the first interesting thing I've seen in months."

We're not married, although our employment visas say we are. She picked me up in a bar one block from the Hamilton courthouse where she finalized her divorce, one hour after I was suspended with pay pending the outcome of the school board's investigation. We talked about teaching, other things. She listened, chose not to judge the blurred line between accusation and conviction. We moved in together a week later, then shifted our lives to Kuwait last year. The school needs bodies at the front of classrooms; they don't background-check too thoroughly.

I've never seen her this excited. She was calm when we met, calm even when we saw the blue line on the pregnancy test a couple months later. Calm when she spoke about naming her stillborn daughter Lily, about the broomstick her ex-husband used on her still-swollen belly, screaming that he wouldn't let her kill any more babies. She was calm through our miscarriage, telling me it was better not to have met Echo, our in-utero code name for the baby. There were a few days of bleeding and expelled pieces of foetal tissue and we tried to act as normal as possible, going out for drinks, a few meals, a movie. Later, I said, "Maybe it's my fault, maybe I hit you in my sleep." She looked at me like she could spit. "It has nothing to do with you," she said. "I'm the one who's been flushing bits of Echo down toilets all over town." Kuwait seemed exotic when we signed the contracts, a desert escape to a new kind of heat.

"I thought betting was haram," I say to Dhari.

She rolls her eyes. "You and your efforts to integrate."

Her charade prevents her from using local words and phrases and she's annoyed whenever I try. English is her armour, even when the effort it takes is comical. "The chopped up salad with parsley and tomato and onion," she'll say to the pained waiters. "Barbecued meat, flatbread, chickpea spread." Never kebab, never schwarma, never hummus.

"Is betting really prohibited here?" she asks. "So many things are."

Dhari makes a waving motion with one hand, as if to say, Nothing is totally forbidden. He asks, "How much were you thinking of investing?"

Investing, I think. Strange word.

"How much did we bring, Dan? Enough?"

"Thirty, forty dinars," I say.

Dhari laughs. "Not nearly enough, my friend."

"There's a minimum price?"

"Oh, yes."

The men have taken their seats again, and a small army of dark-skinned servers emerges from somewhere to serve refreshments. Conversation swells excitedly and we're ignored, Edie's misdemeanours forgotten. She refuses the food and drink and looks at the dates being dipped into camel's milk. Shudders theatrically.

"God, I hope that's pasteurized," she says.

I've sat cross-legged with Dhari in musty Bedouin tents so I know that the milk is warm and fresh, a desert tradition. I want to apologize again for her, but this time make Dhari hear it. I might apologize for everything, right back to when she insisted on accompanying me into the men's lounge over my whispered protests. She just snorted. "You'll probably ask me to put on a burqa next." That was the first wrong thing she said.

Dhari slaps me on the shoulder and leans forward excitedly.

"Now for the real race," he says.

The camels are paraded in front of the viewing stand in a long line. There are no robots this time. Instead, young boys ride atop the animals on full saddles and tack, waving timidly to the grandstand. Around us, the men point and chatter at the mounts, no doubt making boasts and laying claim. The boys are no more than four or five years old, tiny things with legs like matchsticks bouncing against the flanks of their animals. Now the day makes sense, the strict security at the gate, the presence of only purebred Kuwaitis aside from Edie and me. Just a notch higher on my new friend's list of things he loves that aren't quite legal. I thought he was bragging when he spoke of whores and hashish, anything I want.

I hear myself saying something stupid about the legality of boy jockeys.

"Yes, but you can buy one from me, if you wish," Dhari says. "Perhaps next time—if you bring more money."

"I just wanted us to have a nice day away from the apartment," I say.

The boys and the camels are led away to the start line, barely visible across a stretch of bright, hard desert. I turn towards Edie to apologize. Chattering away to Dhari about the jockeys, she doesn't hear. She wonders aloud, her voice low and calm, how common it is to find them in private homes.

MOM 2 MOM

CAM DOESN'T REALLY mind driving me around to these things. He looks at home behind the wheel of the ancient Ford Ranger his father sold him after he quit the army. Likes to talk about the Ranger's good mileage, how his father took such good care of the engine that it still sings even after thirty years. Most days he takes his lunch—always a ham sandwich with one slice of processed cheese and a can of Coors—to the garage, slides the driver's seat way back, and listens to his old high school CDs on the new stereo deck, the only change he's made. I've learned not to ask him to come inside—it's his place, but even after a few weeks I still wonder which drawers are mine.

"No, go ahead," he says. "Text me when you're done."

"You could come in—there's nothing nearby anyhow."

"I'll find a coffee shop or something."

"The last sale had a table with donuts and everything."

He rubs his thumb along the buffed vinyl arc of the steering wheel, shakes his head, and tells me to have fun. I lean across and give him a kiss on the cheek. As he drives away, through the smudged glass on the back of the cab I see the silhouette of his hand come up to his face, although I can't tell if it's just resting there or wiping something away. I smell a vaporous remnant of his shaving cream on the damp March air.

This is the third *Mom 2 Mom* sale I've been to in as many weeks but the one I'm most excited about. The women at the other sales gush about the selection and the number of sellers who show up here. *If you get to any of them*, they say, *make sure you hit Grace Baptist out past Waterdown. They're making babies on production lines over there. Must be something in the water.* The pregnant ones always rub their bellies when they say it, a hungry gesture I can't quite match. I'm a petite five months and barely showing at all.

I turn towards the church. It's a new building, all straight lines and gentle angles and perched on its own small hill, the property fronting Concession Road #3. On one side, dark woods brood over a stream on the property line. The other two sides are shored up by the berms the municipality uses to hide the adjacent landfill from the road, but from the church's gravel parking lot everything is on full display. Bulldozers push mounds of trash bags to the edge of the built-up ground and later cover them with earth, raising flocks of panicked seagulls with each change of direction.

"Hi! Welcome to Grace!"

A perky waif in tight jeans and blonde highlights is waiting behind a table just beyond the front doors, her hand already extended, palm up. The cardboard sign next to the girl says that the sale is free, but that there's a recommended donation of five dollars. The sales are always fundraisers, either for church programs or distant charities that sound vaguely familiar. I uncrumple a greasy bill from my pocket and hand it over. In return, I'm given a plastic bag that will be filled with pregnancy swag like yoga and diet pamphlets, vitamin samples, maternity store coupons, and the like.

"Have you been to a *Mom 2 Mom* sale before?" she asks.

She gives me a scan, her eyes stopping at my belly. This seems to be part of the rite-of-passage at these sales, even from the young and definitely un-pregnant, followed by the requisite questions and necessary platitudes. *How far along are you? How are you feeling? What's the date? Boy or girl? You look great! You're glowing!* I wonder if she even knows she's doing it, and then wonder if my lack of a baby bump will register. In my mind, she'll ask, *Are you even expecting?* and I'll struggle to find a gracious response, her question like sandpaper grit between my teeth. Like a few days ago when Cam came in from the garage and asked, "How do I know it's even mine?" I gnashed my teeth about trust and offered to pay for a DNA test, called a cab to go to the clinic, then fought with Cam as the cabbie spun ruts in the spring-soft driveway when we told him he wasn't needed after all.

"Sure have," I manage to say. "They're great."

As though I've passed some test, her eyes light up. She introduces herself—she's a Madison, of course—and launches into her spiel, punctuated by enthusiastic words she's obviously been coached to say. The sale is a Longstanding Grace Youth Group Tradition, a Fundraiser for a Missions Trip to Uganda to Help The Africans.

"And you'll be going, too?"

"It's my third trip," she says. "They can't even build their own wells or churches."

I start to wish her luck, but her sparkly eyes have already moved on to a pair of hugely pregnant women who've just arrived behind me. I step past her farther into the foyer, which is jammed with tables piled high with all sorts of baby miscellany and staffed by women mostly younger than me but with darker shadows beneath their eyes. The customers are all women, too. They browse between the tables in cheerful bargain packs of two or three, teenagers looking for things to giggle about, moms leading daughters around and purchasing their grandparenthood, Starbucks-toting friend groups in ill-fitting yoga wear with pregnancies carefully aligned.

I stop at a colourful table piled high with winter clothing. I can't resist digging through—it's been organized by age and gender, so each pile is a bright life story, from the impossibly small to the joyously more substantial.

"When are you due?"

The woman sitting on the folding chair behind the table is looking at me over her phone. Her stylish glasses reflect two identical squares of bright blue from the screen.

"Second week in July," I say.

"Oh, you should head into the sanctuary. Lots of newborn stuff there."

"Thanks, I will."

"You won't need these things for a while. My stuff starts at twelve months."

Even after three sales, it's embarrassing how little I

know. The other women seem so wise, something moving through their life stories that hasn't been woven into mine. One of the ladies at the last sale, held at a Christian school in Smithville, paused in the middle of a story about her fourth child, and shook her head. "I never thought I'd have to wait so long for a boy—I'm 29, you know." I'd assumed she was older than me. I left the sale without buying anything, the aging reality of childbearing keeping me in a daze as I walked away. After Cam picked me up, he caught me worrying small bits of vinyl from the Ranger's seat with my fingernail. "Damn it, Yellie, it's hard to find parts for this model. The seat's still the original. Fuck."

Cam doesn't swear very often. It's one of the things that makes him handsome. Sometimes, after he's been on his own for a while, he develops a hard edge, but it always passes quickly. He's soft and firm and polite, which is why I got over my nervousness and spoke to him first after we got off that bus. For the entire trip, his army buddies had been so loud and foul, and he wasn't, and when I said hello and asked if he'd like to get a coffee, he smiled and said yes. He endured the hard time they gave him about abandoning the unit, sat down with me at the GO Terminal café, and missed his connection when I invited him to my tiny apartment above the Sally Ann store on King Street. He got out four months later, with a little money paid out for something that happened overseas, and his first call was to me. I decided that it would be all right for him to know that he got us pregnant. "You're keeping the baby," he said. "That's a good thing." But he said it kind of like a question. A few days later, he found an old house to rent and said I could live there if I wanted to.

I pull out my phone and text him:—*so far so good lots of ppl here*

I tap SEND and move into the sanctuary, a huge space tinted brightly by stained glass windows. Stacks of chairs line the wall, a skyline of dark upholstery. It's packed with tables and women and children darting around. The sound would be the gentle roar of a sideline subway station, but the tasteful taupe carpeting and suspended sound pads dampen it to a self-conscious hush. No one's whispering, but it sounds like they are.

The sound gets me. I've been here before. I raise my hand to my forehead and dig my middle and ring fingers in until it hurts.

"Shit," I say.

"You didn't bring your friend with you this time."

She could be the girl at the front door's older sister, until you see the wrinkles partially filled in with foundation, more than a hint of crow's feet, parenthetical frown lines. I remember the eyes, so pale I can't tell if they're blue or grey. Edged in perfect black eyeliner, stark, bringing out their lightness. Her facial skin tone is at odds with the neck that's visible just above the pink t-shirt's collar and the hands holding a clipboard against her breasts. Black yoga pants, on brand, and pink runners to complete the ensemble. Even the soles of the shoes are pink. Everything looks new.

I hedge, trying to buy a moment. I was here a few years ago, all fucked up and thirsting for adventure, before I grew up. Before grace settled me down and threw me into a job that pays well enough to make permanent change possible, if I line things up just so. I'm waiting for an overdue pay bump and a promotion, and haven't told anyone at work about the pregnancy, although some of the women probably suspect. I want to introduce myself properly, like I can now, so far removed from a time when I lived in clothes so trashy they looked used even in the store.

But my confidence has deserted me, my edge is gone—I'm the impostor again. "I'm sorry, I—do I know you?"

She smirks. "And not British, either. I knew it."

That day was a blur of a friend and me getting lost on our way up Highway 6 to a party in Guelph, weaving into the parking lot to ask directions, ending up inside and playing our roles as a joke, arm in arm. "*Weeah Cock'ney lesbiyins,*" we drawled. "*'Opin' to foind somefink fo' the bay-bay! Nappays and prams, luv—nappays and prams!*" The rest of it so indistinct aside from our brutal accents and the voice of this woman, sharp behind us as we stumbled around the stalls making messes and mocking everyone. She didn't like it when Tamara, as high as I was, leaned in so close she could have licked the lady's lashes. "*Is yo' oy loinah tattew'd on?*" Guessing afterwards, having fled in the car when the police got called and laughing ourselves lost even more, that she must have been one of the organizers. Important somehow. She got her own line of the chant we made up, "*Fucked wif the pahsta's woife, we did!*" as we drove up and down rural roads that all looked the same. Tamara and I are still Facebook friends, but I've blocked her.

"I think you should leave," the pink shoe lady says.

"Look, I'm here alone. I'm due in July, and I didn't realize—"

My phone buzzes. Without thinking, I bring it up and look at Cam's reply:—*ok*

"I don't believe you," she says.

She's scrutinizing my left hand, looking for a wedding band. Her ring finger is festooned with a huge stone and matching gold bands, garish against her pale skin. It's strange what we look at when escape isn't a possibility, and I can't say it with any authority, but I'm certain that aside from the kids everyone else in the sanctuary is married. All I can see is diamonds and gold, princess cut, squares and ovals, flush bezels and posts that grip the stones like four-fingered old hags.

I've never worn rings. I tried my mother's on once when I was just a girl, but it felt so confining that I had to take it off. It was probably just sized too small, but how would I know? For a moment, a band of cool remained on the skin from the alcohol in the cleaning contraption on the bathroom counter, where she'd put the ring in a little basket and drop it in. Mother's ring never left the cleaner —she just faithfully topped up the alcohol every so often as it evaporated. The woman standing in front of me probably never takes hers off, even to do the dishes or sweat through spin class, the skin and muscle underneath proudly compressed. Outfits chosen to match. Makeup, too. Expectations.

This is tiresome, I think, and so predictable.

I put my phone away and fold my arms. "I'm not a ring kind of person."

"I beg your pardon?"

"Like you are, obviously."

She's taken a half step back, clutching the clipboard to her chest with both arms. Looking to both sides for support or escape. I start to feel a bit of the old defiance —who the fuck is she, right?—but it leaves me as quickly as it came, as though the carpet and sound padding absorbed it too. The voice it gave itself was the Oxy voice from not too long ago, ridiculous. "*'Ew the fuck is shay, roight?*" I don't want to fight today.

"I'm sorry. I won't be any trouble."

"No, you won't, because I'm calling the police."

"Okay," I say, although I know she won't this time.

And then my back is to her and I'm wandering past the sale tables, immersed in an ocean of used onesies and sleepers and rompers, wandering a forest of strange torture contraptions for breastfeeding and carrying the tiniest of beings. At every table there's at least one package that never got opened, little jewels amongst all the secondhand items and slightly faded kiddie clothes. I'm amazed at the bargains. A few days ago, Cam drove me to a baby store where the prices left me speechless enough for him to comment on after he picked me up. "You're quiet," he said, and waited for me to fill the space behind his question, getting angry when I didn't, twisting the volume up to drown us both out. Here, though, everything is a fraction of the price in the stores, the items gently used but generally well cared for. It's hopeful how cheap everything is.

A table at the far side of the sanctuary draws me in with its fantastic colour range. Colours I'd wear myself, earth tones and blues and greys, and unexpected combinations you'd swear wouldn't work, but do. Not a dusty pink or powder blue onesie in sight. I lift a sealed package of hemp baby cloths and turn it over, looking for the price.

"Go ahead, take it," the woman behind the table says.

"I'd like to pay."

She waves away my offer. Asks, "First time buying baby washcloths?"

"Any kind of washcloth, in fact."

"You'll get dozens of them. Receiving blankets, too. They're on every what-to-get-the-new-mom list. Seriously, take them, on me."

"Thanks."

I look down at the cloths, thinking about all the people I haven't told. Won't.

"Single mom," she says.

A simple statement of fact, as easy and confident as sunrise. She sits back in her chair, nods, and smiles, lighting up the sunspots and wrinkles on her makeup-free face. No grey hair yet, although I suspect she wouldn't really care either way. Jeans and a wool cardigan. No rings, either.

"Yes. No. He's around," I say.

"That's good."

"And you?"

"No, it's just me and the beans."

"Your kids."

She lifts her chin at the far side of the church, next to the stage, where a young boy is holding court with a handful of other kids his age. He's a born leader, even I can see, with a shabby look and shaggy hair you can tell is the envy of every other child.

"That's Ozzie, bean number one," she says.

"He's popular."

She gives a snort. "Yeah, church kids love him—probably sense he'll be the one with the good weed someday."

I laugh at the surprise and the truth of it. Sudden, sharp, delicious. My cheeks are out of practice.

"And this is Roz, bean two," she says. "Say hello, sweetheart."

She looks down and gives the car seat on the floor next to her a fond, work-booted nudge. I didn't notice the seat before, or the pink nonpareil nested into the blankets there. A tiny, pleased gurgle makes its way past the folds of cloth, and I watch the mother take a deep breath, as though she can fill her lungs with the perfect acceptance radiating from that little face.

"How old?"

"Three months and twenty-four days," she says.

Roz wiggles her nose and falls back asleep with an unexpectedly accomplished groan. And I can't help but think that we're never that still again.

"I'm Yelhemina," I say. "But call me Yellie."

"Liz."

A beat.

"You all have z's in your names."

"You make connections where you can," she says, shrugging.

It's the kind of thing that annoys me, like matching couples' t-shirts or colour schemes for family photographs. But I can tell that Liz isn't the type to reach for cuteness or nicety. No, these names have history, good leftover names you'd dig through old genealogies for, settling on the ones that can bear new weight, too, if you shore them up in just the right way. Oswald, maybe. Rosalind. I don't know where mine came from—I suspect my mother made it up just to have a funny story to tell at the bar.

I feel a presence beside me. The woman with the clipboard has appeared from somewhere and is looking at Liz with exasperation. I'm impressed with how focused she is as she ignores me—I'd say she's pretending I'm not there, but it's more like her mind can actually make me not exist.

"I've asked you to speak to your son about his language."

"Why, what'd he say?"

There's a smirk on Liz's face. She waits a long moment for the woman to respond, savouring the possibility that her response might include the language in question.

"He said the *d-word*," the woman finally whispers.

"Damn, you mean. He said damn."

"Liz, please."

"I just want to be precise."

"Liz—"

"All right, all right, I'll talk to him again."

"Soon, okay?"

With the precision of a drill sergeant, the woman turns on her heel—away from me, even though it's the more awkward move—and walks primly away. Liz watches her go, slides her gaze back to me, intrigued.

"There's a story there," she says.

So I give her the dime tour, from underestimating the Oxy two years ago to the threat of calling the police earlier today. I throw in some extras, too, like how getting pregnant makes me worry about my job and that I'll have to make a stark adjustment to my make-it-right program, how Cam seems to be strong but it's still easy to worry about him, how I have this feeling his stillness has to do with what happened to him overseas, how I think he'll probably never tell me. I finish by saying I didn't recognize the church until I came into the sanctuary.

"And Vicky saw you right away, I'm sure."

"That's her name? It fits."

"Oh, she's a peach, all right," she says, and chuckles. "Well, that's my church word for her, anyhow."

"You go here?"

"When I can, yes. There's lots of kids for Ozzie to play with."

I'm surprised. Somewhere in my past, church had never been presented as something you fit into life, but much more the other way around. And for her to be a single mother with kids years apart, one of whom is a newborn, well, that must be a story too. Churches and single parents—especially women—are oil and water. I ask how long she's been a member.

"I'm not one, although they'd love it if I were," she says. "I started coming when I found out I was pregnant with Roz. They've been good to me."

"How do they accept, you know—" I raise my left hand and waggle my empty ring finger.

She laughs and admits that the math is complicated from a faith-community standpoint. She was married when Ozzie was born, the result of a Las Vegas wedding chapel fling with a very fertile American army officer. They ended things soon afterwards but he never filed divorce papers. A month or so after he was vaporized on a roadside in Iraq, she found out that she was entitled to the survivor benefits. Roz was a much later surprise, of course, from one night of trying to remember what being a woman felt like. She hasn't told the father.

"I just say I'm a widow, most of the time," she says. "And I am, technically, but not because of that IED."

A strange thing to say, I think.

"It keeps people from trying too hard to set me up, too," she says, as though reading my thoughts.

There's a buzz from my pocket:—*r u done?*

Cam always tells me to take my time, have fun, that he'll be fine, but he's impatient. Like the time runs away from him when he's alone and it freaks him out. Aside from that one night, we've only been together a few weeks, but he always texts me when he feels the rush, like he'll catch it if he can just put me back in the passenger seat, help buckle me in. He brought me to meet his father right after he found out about the baby. Had a vision and everything, one where he finds an excuse to leave his father and me alone in that musty house and we bond. "Call me Terry," were the old man's first words, before offering me a cognac. "Let's have a chat." Cam disappeared up to his old bedroom. Not fifteen minutes later, right in the middle of Terry's photo memory tour, untouched cognac warming against my palm, my phone thrummed in my pocket. The same words as today:—*r u done?*

Liz glances at the phone. She looks like she knows about impatience. "Hey, it was great talking with you."

"You too."

"Ozzie!" she yells across the sanctuary.

Heads turn and shake at the disturbance. Ozzie detaches himself from his admiring crowd and heads over.

Liz starts grabbing onesies and sleepers and other bits of earth-toned, gender neutral baby-wear and stuffs them into a greenish shopping bag. The cloths get placed on top. She grabs a roll of masking tape and scribbles on it with a sharpie she has tucked into her jeans pocket. Peels it away from the roll and, with a deft wrist snap, tears the tape and sticks it to the cellophane around the baby cloths.

"Looks like I'll get to make one tag today after all," she says.

"I can't accept this," I say. "What about Roz—she'll need these things."

She shakes her head, waves my words away somewhere. There's no space for argument—my objections are just gone, gone, gone. Nods at the tape tag. "That's my cell number, if you ever feel like getting dragged to church."

I reach for the bag, my hand travelling to my non-existent belly.

"We'll tell everyone it's an immaculate conception," she says, smiling.

"Just like yours," I say.

"Exactly like mine. Right, Oz?"

Ozzie grins shyly. "Right, Mom."

"This is Ms. Yellie."

"Hi."

"Can you carry this for her out to her car?"

"Aww, I was just—"

"Either that or you carry everything we don't sell today. All your old stuff. All. Of. It."

"Fine," he says, dramatically seizing the looped handles and heading for the exit.

I reach out a hand to shake hers, but she's leaning

down and reaching for the carseat. I can't really know, but I think there's a good possibility she's softly running a mother's finger across a baby daughter's cheek. I've heard that if you close your eyes and cast off the world for an instant you can actually feel love tingling through the downy hairs on a newborn's face. I don't buy it, though.

On my way out of the sanctuary, I text Cam and tell him I'm ready to go. I pass Vicky and Madison at the donations table—there's no doubt now that they're mother and daughter—but they don't notice me. Ozzie's at the glass doors at the front of the church, looking at all the cars and trucks in the parking lot, his feet far apart and swinging the bag forward and back between them.

He asks, "Is that your truck?"

"No, he'll be here soon, I—"

But it is the Ranger after all, its thirty-year-old red paint bright against the grey of the lot's crushed gravel. Idling in the small turnaround, waiting for me like I'm an old lady who needs a pickup after a hymn-sing. Cam's behind the wheel, looking through the windshield at the trash-movers growling across the muddy property next door. As Ozzie and I walk out, ducking our heads in the futile attempt to ward away the rain that has started to fall, I can see Cam's hands at ten and two, tapping slowly to some tune on the CD player I can't hear. He has the volume down—normally I'd hear the thrum and bass of the speakers through the truck's thin skin.

"Thanks, Ozzie, I can—"

"I got it."

"No, you can go back to your friends, and—"

"I said I *GOT* it."

He reaches out and tugs at the old door latch, clunking it open and swinging the door carefully out with one hand, balancing the plastic bag in the other. I hear him and Cam trade Hellos as he heaves the bag into the footwell with a satisfied grunt. He stands to the side as I slide into the seat, looking concerned and with a hand partway out, as though it's enough to be close to my elbow in case of emergency. His actions are undertaken smoothly, without the smallest portion of self-consciousness. Familiar.

"Can you thank your mother for me?" I ask.

"Sure."

"I think the baby will like the stuff your mother gave us."

"Yeah, it's my old blankets and my socks and my jammies. From a box in my closet. They're yours now."

Cam taps the steering wheel, coughs, and shifts in his seat. Ozzie reaches to the edge of the door and looks at me.

"Are you all inside?"

"I am. You're a real gentleman," I say, and mean it.

"Mom always asks for my help."

"You're good at it, too."

He shrugs. "There are lots of trucks around."

And he shuts the door, in the end having to use both hands to slam it past the catch in the hinge. Once the door closes, the noise from Cam's stereo deck faintly fills the cab, almost too soft to hear yet recognizable too, a song from his favourite classic rock mixed CD. Track number thirteen, I know, just like I'm starting to know that Cam won't start singing until the third verse, right after the guitar solo.

We pull away. From the corner of my eye I see that

Ozzie hasn't moved, that he's standing on the gravel with his arms folded, staring after the truck as it leaves. I can't stop myself from grabbing the rearview mirror and turning it so I can watch him and the parking lot fade behind us on our way to the main road. So I can watch Ozzie and realize that he's wearing old black gumboots far too large for him, see him watch us until we turn onto the concession road. He'll nod at a job well done, and head back to the sanctuary, I just know it.

"Nice kid," Cam says after a few minutes.

"Nice kid," I reply.

He leaves the volume down as we drive. The Ranger's tires hiss through the shallow puddles spotting the old concession road and roar through the deeper ones. I lean forward, grab the bag from the cool footwell, and hold it tight against myself, compressing the clothing inside by crossing both arms. I imagine its warmth through my own clothing, the cottons and wools and synthetics holding their heat well, as the scenery flashes past in a blur of greys and greens and browns.

It's awhile before I say anything. "I don't think I want to do this with you."

"No, it's not something I want, either."

Cam drives and we listen to the CD almost all the way through. Eventually my hands grow cold and I slide them under my thighs, just inches from the sharp edge in the vinyl I made with my thumbnail after the last sale. I don't think Cam would swear at me again, not now, but it's better to give my hungry hands somewhere safe to rest.

FAIRLY TRADED

HANNAH ALWAYS SITS on the tall stool so her right side faces the window or the door. The shiny pamphlet the American corpsman thrust into her hand when she was discharged had a whole panel dedicated to the effectiveness of sunscreen for scars. Master Corporal Blanchard, her 2IC, a man with an ex, a baby daughter he never sees, and a wives' tale for every occasion, snorted when he saw it.

"They tell you that shit to keep the sunscreen makers happy," he said.

"So it isn't true."

"Fuck, no. You want scars to fade, blast 'em with sun."

Blanchard was wrong. Took a couple of months of sunburns and itchiness and the beginnings of a strange brown hue for the truth to bite, but there it is. Sun is really fucking bad for scars, especially the ones you aren't ready for. Hannah has also discovered that the scars are usually colder than her other skin, too, so the sunlight reflecting from the granite floor feels nice. Warms the right side of her face and her arm almost enough to forget the cold. Forget the tiny bits of ground and metal that still appear in her sheets most mornings. Works through the skin. For a lifetime.

"Another Sumatran?"

Hannah looks up from her laptop. Olson stands there, a pristine bar towel slung over his left shoulder, the hardest barista ever to sling espresso. Squinting behind fashionably thick eyeglass frames far too effete for a trooper who had likely sent more than a few hajis directly to paradise. Misses the uniform, maybe, reckons that hipster wear is a suitable substitute. His limp an ironic accessory.

"Sure, why not? Where am I gonna go, right?"

He takes her mug, grinds the necessary grams of whole bean, slow-drips her coffee, and clicks a toonie onto the dark wooden bar next to her laptop.

"The fuck's that for?"

"You won't take my discount, Doc, you get a rebate every tenth cup. House rules."

Hannah doesn't argue. Not clever enough, refusing his vet discount, hoping her spot at the coffee bar was hers to pay full price for. She looks over at the clear tip bowl and wonders if she could sneak it in there, camouflaged by a few other toonies. No joy—mostly empty, only silver.

"New tat, O?"

"Yep."

He looks down at the jagged line on his forearm, edged in angry red. You'll never get war stories out of him, but he'll parade those tattoos around like they're kin. Hannah checked him out, called in a couple of favours at NDHQ in Ottawa—field medics get all sorts of promises, something about saving lives and debts owed—and found out Olson is as hard as they come. Blacked out lines in files, units that don't exist, places no one's supposed to be. Et cetera. There was a quiet day, months ago, when she was alone in the shop, when she called him on it.

"You were there. The sandbox."

He looked at her through those glasses and nodded. "You got some under your skin, too, I think."

He wasn't looking for patrol stories, just why she limped into his shop every day to do battle with her gun-metal grey laptop. So Hannah told him about a vaccination clinic in a village outside the wire, the infantry being committed elsewhere, the old Soviet hand grenade squeezed between the window covers and bouncing off her right leg. How it only half exploded. How the scars, on account of the body armour, ended at her right hip and began again at her throat. Their coolness and how they always felt brand new. About how the pension for a severed foot wasn't enough but how a lost right eye made the payout worthwhile.

"So now I freelance, even though my depth perception is fucked."

"Fucking war paid for everything, eh?"

"You could say that, yeah. How about you?"

His eyes were solid, respectful, as he slid her coffee in front of her. "Titanium hip. AK round on exfil. Tats are patrol maps for ops where we lost Buddy. Payout helped pay for the shop."

Twenty-two words, heavy enough to make her know where her coffee would always come from. Called his new adventure The Wadi Cafe, specializes in fair trade coffee and tea. Heavy, indeed, like the honour of a man who'd seen and been dealt hell yet still cared about coffee pickers he'd never meet. How he evangelized about the preservation of livelihood and living wages. Tributes. How the tattoos spidered over his arms like dark veins, how many there were. How customers felt free to tell him their own lame tattoo tales, never knowing the chasm between drunken frat ink and Olson's honour tats. That's when he started calling her Doc—the troops always did—but they never talked about the war again.

There's a commotion in the corner. A squeal of pure delight from a chubby regular with greasy hair and an oversized Transformers ball cap as he takes a boxed toy from the new guy across the table. They've covered the table with a menagerie of toys still in their boxes. Chubby guy hands over a wad of bills without taking his eyes from his prize. They don't look like they know each other yet you can see a chemistry there, thirty-something introverts sensing whom it's safe to hang out with. And where.

Olson watches them fondly as he wipes down the gleaming red enamel on the LaMarzocco on the bar. "Those toys never come out of their boxes."

She sips her coffee and sits back on the barstool, looking at the images on her screen. A digital livelihood now. Sandstorm free. There's the habit of dropping Fuck into every conversation like punctuation, sometimes forgetting that not everyone does. Scanning for alleys and crannies along every street in case it all goes lateral. Distance. From before the war until now.

Flirting with the reserves on weekends helped pay for design school, but a tough startup market practically volunteered her for active duty. Isolation pay and nothing to spend it on helped her put some away with a dream of restarting that business, but the terror made her count days and hours until the roto was over. That dud grenade just sealed the decision to get back to freelancing, although a few months of rehab at the NATO hospital in Germany had forced her to wait. Cold scars and a limp are her legacy, far easier to bear than the suicides and shattered marriages the other pamphlets warn about.

"Wife and kid?"

"They're good, Doc, thanks for asking."

"Danny must getting big."

A smile, quick and sharp as shrapnel. "Little fucker's already smarter than the wife and me combined."

He says The Wife with affection, rather than the cold distance most men give it. Ball and Chain. Old Lady. Not Olson—Buddy is all edge and angle but soft with respect for the woman who stayed long after she could have left. Hannah turns slightly and takes a long look at the closed shop door and the splash of sunlight off the granite, trying to imagine who might come through next. Watching the shadows flit by on the sidewalk, thinking it would be all right if one of them interrupted her warming light, maybe bought her dinner. No one does.

"Fuck it. Back to work," she says.

But it feels better when her feet are on the ground, so she stands and looks for a free spot at a table. She closes her laptop and drawing tablet and tucks them under her left arm, warming her ribcage. She takes hold of the mug with her trigger finger and lifts it towards Olson in a quick salute. He doesn't see or respond, absorbed by lining up the tiny espresso cups on top of the machine in precise white ranks.

The chair beside the rough barn board table tucked against the wall is cool through her jeans. She puts everything onto the rough surface and sits, right side to the window. The screen brightens, revealing a stylized human heart she designed to be worked like a puzzle. She's on deadline for a half dozen scalable diagrams for a med school e-text her new friend Gav bid on. He runs a small design boutique around the corner from The Wadi. Contracted her with a handshake precisely four minutes after catching sight of her work. He'd been waiting for his cappuccino, she'd been diagramming for a wetlands conservation website, a lot of ducks and ponds and innumerable shades of green. The heart's a far more interesting project, driven by the vision of tired med students disassembling and reassembling her body parts on their laptops. Tired but intact, nothing but brightness ahead of them.

Gav's late. She fidgets with her mug and moves heart bits around and tries not to look at the clock at the top of the screen. Tries to ignore the phantom pain in her absent foot. The surgeons warned her about residual sensation, as they called it, which could manifest as itching or burning or pain. Her own version? The tension and roughness of the field dressing Blanchard tied too tight as blood gushed through the mess where her foot and ankle had been. That's what she still feels, even though they amputated six inches below the knee, three inches above where the damn dressing had been. "Good tibia," they said. "Positive outcome for prosthesis." Good tibia. The part you got to keep, anyhow.

At their first meeting, Gav didn't flinch when she explained the limp. Her heart did, though, two minutes into that first conversation when she realized he wasn't staring at the scars or the slightly drunk way her right eye wandered. Just listening. She tries not to swear so much around him.

The toy guys yell a quick thanks to Olson and nearly bowl Gav over as he holds the door open for them. He sees her and smiles. She hates that she's already blushing. Hates even more that she wants to stare at him as he rounds the table and sits on her right, slightly blocking the warming light she suddenly doesn't need.

Olson's on it.

"The usual?"

"Skim milk for this one. Have to watch my figure," Gav says laughing.

Olson ducks behind the machine, frowning, his inner barista disdainful of a cappuccino made with anything other than whole milk. She doesn't mind. *Buddy who takes care of himself is Good Buddy.* Gav's Good Buddy. She'd let him take care of himself for a lifetime.

"You've made some progress on the heart," he says, nodding at her screen.

"Once you find vector points for each part, it comes together easier."

"Yeah, I've found that, too."

They talk shop for a few minutes. He wants to know about her progress and plans and timelines, things she can reply to automatically. After Olson delivers the cappuccino they sit and work in silence for a while. She can tell that Gav has to work harder on the images than she does. Hates that he won't be able to teach her anything. He'd be a good teacher, patient as he is. It's hard to ask for help, sometimes. Harder still to ask for what you really, really want.

Her laptop blinks itself into the screen saver, startles both of them. Quick darkness then the swirl and dance of a digital aurora borealis created for some unknown sky.

"Sorry," she says. "Don't know where I went there."

"I'm not paying you to dream, Hannah."

She apologizes again, not catching the playfulness in his tone. He lays his left hand on her forearm, light and quick, a bird wing apology against flight. A brief flaring of sensation from her absent limb and a few other places, the urge to cup the back of his neck with a perfectly curved palm. But he's looking at his computer, assembling his parts—he has the skeleton, put himself in charge of the bones—and doesn't see her sudden brightening. A long moment passes, one in which he doesn't rise, sweep her off her whatever.

Fuck it, Troop, get yours.

"We should go out," she says.

"Mmm? Yeah, let's do the next one somewhere else."

"No, I mean, let's just go out. Leave the laptops at home."

Mock horror on his beautiful face. "Leave them at home? That'd be like cutting off—"

Realization. Mortification. An arm? A leg? A life, maybe?

"God, Hannah, I'm so sorry, I didn't think."

And there it is. Buddy's a step below brave after all. Below perfect. *Take charge, medic, assess the scene, triage the casualties.* A brief career of calming men in unthinkable moments—humour can heal, confidence can cover anything, distraction is key—takes over.

"Fuckers only sent one fucking boot back with me, you believe that shit?"

He doesn't say anything, just drags his eyes along the scars on her neck and arms and towards her feet as though he could see the composites and light metals through her shoe. Dropping Fuck into conversation again, as though everyone does it. As though she could know why or explain. About any of it. He sits back, rubs the back of his head, sighs loudly.

"Hey, Gav, no big deal, right? Let's just—"

"No, I should've told you. I'm married. Maybe you can meet—I've told him all about you."

A beat. She snorts out loud. "Gay and married. The perfect storm."

No re-do here. He cringes and starts to gather his things, his shaking hands tidying up the pieces of what had been a nice day. There are words of some kind. From him. She just folds her arms and watches him stand, her ears almost too hard to hear his offer to meet the next day, same time, same place. Lip reads his attempt to reassure her that nothing needs to change, the contract is still valid, the deadlines are still creeping. Doesn't feel the pink mist of their friendship covering them both as easily as the pieces of her foot covered the walls of that dusty room near Kandahar.

Doesn't say goodbye. *Never say goodbye. Never tell them they're dying. Buddy won't be ready to hear it, ever.*

Slowly, slowly, she gathers her own things, packing them away in reverse order, the order she will need them next. The collar of her prosthetic feels cool against the stump. It healed perfectly, much to the pride of the surgeons and therapists who kept telling her how much they saved. Good tibia. At least they'd never tried to tell her how lucky she was, how good things would be—they'd seen too many paths like hers to put faith in bullshit. She slings her work satchel across her shoulders, loops her fingers through the mug handles, brings them to the counter. Olson limps over and takes the mugs. He opens his mouth to speak but closes it, moving over to the dishwasher without a sound.

She wonders if maybe he sees how pale she is, how tight her shoulders, the deeper lines on her face, the extra movement of the glass eye when she's tired or stressed. Maybe he sees in her good eye the absence of anything approaching certainty. In the other, a hole where hope should be. Or maybe sees her look at the tip bowl, turning his broad shoulders away so she can swear extra loud, scoop out all the coins and cram them into her pocket. Life to live, after all. Limp out onto the sidewalk, turning right to go up James Street, looking for places to hide.

THOSE DAYS
JUST A GLIMMER

WHEN DESMOND SHOT that fucker through the eye, he thought his second career was finished. Whether or not his eyes actually took in a wire and a trigger became important only after the kid fell, after everyone else drew their sidearms, after the Primary was hustled into the back of the Yukon and spun away in a cloud of dust. Then Desmond and Tillman advanced on the body, weapons trained on centre of mass, with Desmond already wondering whether he'd done the right thing. Drill the wrong Arab on a private detail, there's no consular protection.

He didn't need it. The kid was maybe eleven, not a hair on his unmarked face, but the Semtex vest under his dishdasha was an adult's toy. Desmond stepped around his blood and brains still pumping onto the asphalt and secured the trigger. Tillman said, "You're gonna be a fucking superstar, Dez," then spoke into his radio. Ten minutes later the Kuwaiti police arrived and took over. They laughed at the smell—the kid shat himself when he died—and simply cut the wires without calling a bomb squad or anything.

That was about a year ago. Tillman was right. Now Desmond has trajectory again. Chooses his assignments and leads the teams. Former officers and sergeants-major asking his opinion. Heady. Lish is proud of him, he can see, even through the nauseating stop-start motion on the web-cam. She's at her folks' place, a tidy ranchhouse surrounded by vineyards Desmond can't stand looking at. Hard to be home alone sometimes. She tut-tuts under her breath when he starts to complain about the routine, the boredom.

"Only you love the excitement," she says. "The rest of us just worry."

He laughs and wiggles his fingers at the baby. Kid can hold his head up now, sits on Lish's lap like a tiny, pixelated king.

"Don't worry, Plug," Desmond says. "Daddy'll be home before you can fill your next diaper."

"Fat chance. And stop calling him that."

"Just a couple more weeks, babe. The company's good about time off."

"Not soon enough."

"Yeah."

"You have a busy day today?"

"Nah. Slow."

Code-speak. Can't talk about where he's going or who they're escorting. Slow means a milk run, lots of guys, low risk. A busy day takes fewer guys into rougher areas. And he just lied to her about when he's coming home—they scheduled a political conference at the last minute, so his freedom-flight will be a week later than they've been planning for. Safer for everyone involved when there's no time for the bad guys to plan, but he's still figuring out how to tell her. She left him when he finally got out of the army but chose to sign right up with a private firm working out of Baghdad. "I can't take any more of the uncertainty," she said. "Can't you find work at home?" They fell back together when he was home on holidays. There was always chemistry there. And now, a baby. The company gave him time off and flew him home when Lish came due. Plug being an affectionate term, but it also keeps him from having to say Jaxson. Lost that argument—what kind of name is that anyway?

Tillman pokes his head into Desmond's room and flashes five fingers, mouths the words, *Five mikes*. Sees the laptop open, puts his head into the frame.

"Hey, Lish," he says. "Jesus, the little fucker's getting big!"

"Language, Andrew!" she says, but she's laughing.

"Gotta take your boy out for awhile," he says.

"Yeah, I have to go," Desmond says.

"Be safe," she says.

"Always."

"I'm loving you," Lish says.

"Loving you back."

"*Loving you back*," Tillman mimics in a falsetto after Desmond closes the computer. "God, you're fucking pathetic."

"Kiss my ass. Gotta keep the wife happy."

Can't tell Tillman that there's no gratitude stronger than that given for a second chance. That it bothers him when the boys give their women hard names. Tillman calls his girlfriend, a tiny thing who sends him care packages every week, My Bitch. He thinks it's cool, caring even, but Desmond thinks it just sounds like the distance between respect and loss. But when you lean on each other every day to stay alive, you blend. You take the jokes and make a few of your own, you laugh at the regs that say you can't fraternize with the local women. You make the occasional visit to the illegal brothels in the city, make jokes about that, too. *What happens in the sandbox stays in the sandbox.*

"Get the boys up," Desmond tells him, even though he knows they're waiting in the vehicle bay.

It's the rituals that save you. A signal to the guys that says, *Time to get serious.* He double checks his load, weapon, ammo. Today brings a two-vehicle run into Mirqab so some sheikh can file some paperwork with another anonymous government ministry. At the door to the garage, he pauses, his fear stopping him, as it always does before they head out. Not of dying, but of not shooting the next godless fool who wants to disassemble them with high explosives or the spray of a Kalashnikov.

It's hard to shake off legend. "The right eye, Dez," Tillman said when he found him puking in the alley. "You put a 10mm round through his fucking right eye from twenty metres. God himself wouldn't have made that shot." He told him to shut up about it, that it was just the training, that any one of them could have. It's not true, though. You don't try distance with a handgun. Maybe you could reach through the long barrel of a properly sighted rifle and touch a fucker that way.

Tillman comes out of the bay, gives Desmond a nod that says we're good to go, closes the door behind him. Looks at Desmond's hands. "Y'all haven't popped yet."

"Nope."

He digs out a small ziplock baggie with a pastel palette of pills inside, fingers out a mint-green one, drops it in Desmond's hand. He downs it dry, winces at the bitter chalk of the aftertaste. He doesn't even ask what Tillman supplies anymore. Fucker made it a priority to get connected as soon as they set up shop in Kuwait, ended up making friends with a distant relative of the Emir who works Customs at the airport. The military supplied the best stuff on deployment but it's harder to come by now that they're private. Stims. Uppers. Downers. Blinders. Pain narcotics. A few of the guys shake, others need help sleeping. They all jump a bit too soon at loud noises and look at walls rather than talk about anything. Tillman just shrugs about the uncertainty of the meds. *Anything you can do to feel different*, he'd probably say.

Desmond and Tillman came up together, although Tillman always liked trouble and has always been a rank behind. Grew up in the same city, went to competing high schools, did battle on the same football and rugby fields but never met before the army. The recruiting officer recommended them for the same unit. Then it was the same schools and deployments, right through UN duty and eventually Afghanistan. Tillman is a legendary scrounger —he can get anything for you if you don't mind not asking too many questions—so he's good to have around. They got out together, too, and saw the same uncertainty when they tried to imagine an After the Army.

Tillman punches Desmond in the arm, slides his sunglasses into place. "Let's go fuck some shit up."

But those days, all those questions they never had to answer, are just a glimmer.

"Tillman—"

"Right, right. Hearts and minds. What I meant to say was, Let's go hide behind our Oakleys for a few hours."

"Keep it tight, Troop."

"Tight as fuck," Tillman says.

❧

They blast through Kuwait City in three black Yukons, lights flashing, as the locals and imported labourers scramble to get out of the way. Windows up, AC roaring against the 120-degree heat. Shiny armoured beetles, Desmond thinks, and smiles at his faint, warped reflection on the inside of the window. The pill was some kind of feel-good, giving the dun-coloured buildings and dusty roads a nice, easy glow.

Fucking milk run, he thinks.

After high school, between graduation and his induction ceremony, he and Lish got high every day. He just stopped smoking and popping pills a few days before reporting for induction. The medic who took his sample and asked all those standard questions shook his head when Desmond admitted that his piss might not be completely clean. "Stay away from that shit from now on, Recruit—officers' random tests aren't usually random," he said. Lish got pissed when Desmond refused to smoke or do pills when he was home on leave. He just said no again and again rather than telling her he actually wanted to stay clean for service, that he was killing all the lectures and drill and exercises in the bush. Saying something like, *I don't need the drugs, it's a new high for me,* sounded weak even though it was true. Panjwaii fucked all that up. He hit Lish once when she snuck up and hugged him from behind. Told the army shrink about it, was given sleep-aids and anxiety meds and a Costco-sized bottle of uppers. *So you can stay sharp*, were the words used.

The first stop is a palace along the Gulf to pick up the sheikh. After we pull up, Tillman looks at our orders again, says that the guy is a grandson of the emir who has his finger on all the telecommunications in the country, from cell phones to car radios to the world wide web. Desmond watches a huge Egyptian bodyguard dressed in a tailored suit come poke his head into the middle vehicle and nod at the palace's front door. The Primary is a short, obese Kuwaiti dressed in an impossibly white dishdasha and starched, red-checked gutra. His alligator shoes are a perfect match for the slim briefcase in his hand. Bright, but the pills make him even brighter. He glows a cheery glow, like the roads and cars and filthy waters of the Gulf.

Tillman, on the wheel, angles his eyes to the side mirrors, waiting for all the doors to close. The Kuwaiti slides into the black leather interior, frowning at some bit of dust or grit on the seat. *Clunk, clunk*, go the doors. There's a burst of scratchy all-clears on the radios and Tillman eases out onto Gulf Street, eyes straight ahead as he accelerates. Desmond, riding shotgun, scans the other vehicles and the imported labourers clustered around the bus stops.

"Land Cruiser, eleven o'clock," he says into the radio. "Tarp covering something in the back."

Everyone tenses up. Sounds like someone else talking, even to his own ears. Years of conditioning taking control from the chemical haze, clearing his vision. *Wired clean,* they used to say when they talked about still being able to get shit done, even hopped up and down and sideways on all that pharmaceutical help dosed out from sterile, dustless blister-packs. Desmond moves his hand to his knee, inches from the submachine gun clipped beneath the dash. The tarp shifts when the Land Cruiser swerves around something in the road.

"Sheep," he says. "It's just a sheep."

"All fucking clear," Tillman says to himself, low, under his breath.

"We might see many of them today," the Kuwaiti says, glancing up from his phone. "Eid Al-hadha is coming soon."

Slaughter-Fest, they called it in Afghanistan. It seemed like every male old enough to hold a knife had dropped everything for a day of slitting sheep throats in honour of some sacrifice to Allah that Ibrahim was supposed to have made. Or was it Ishmael? Desmond can never remember those details, even though he's been surrounded by Arabs for years now. He remembers the temporary markets set up to sell sheep for the festival, though, concrete details like temporary pens erected with steel fencing, the bleating from dry sheep mouths, the animals' spray-painted sides, the barking of the sellers, the panicked buyers fearful of missing out. He imagines marked up prices, like what the gas companies do back home just before long weekends.

"You'll want to slow down through Mirqab," the Kuwaiti says. "It's a busy place. Plenty of workers."

"Thank you, sir," Tillman says. "I will."

"You wouldn't want to dent your vehicles after all."

The Kuwaiti laughs at his own joke without interrupting the rhythm of his thumbs on the touchscreen. His voice is a clipped British accent, a payoff from the billions of dinars the government pays its citizens to educate themselves abroad. Desmond and Tillman glance at each other, mouth the words *Fucking Arabs* before returning their eyes to their quadrants to scan for threats. Desmond swallows the urge to laugh out loud, feels it flutter down his oesophagus like a moth.

His phone thrums against his thigh. A text from Lish, her contact photo flickering onto the scratched and dusty screen.

—*WTF Dezzy? Talked 2 Jen. An xtra fucking wk?*

No one else gets to do this, pull a phone out in the middle of a run to check messages. But this is Desmond's show, so he can do what the fuck he wants. Still, this time he wishes he hadn't.

"You were gonna wait to tell Jen," he says. "Lish is pissed at me now."

"Jesus, that was fast," Tillman says. "Bitches got, like, ESP or something—"

"Tillman—"

"Shit, Dez, she dragged it outta me just before we left base. What was I supposed to do?"

Desmond shakes his head. On Skype the other day, Lish read a few sentences about trust and a lack of secrets from some book on marriage she ordered online. But of course a marriage has to keep secrets, especially a military one. Can't regale the family with stories of the things high-velocity weapons and IEDs do to a body, all those holes and pieces and shredded meat. You have to learn to

talk about it without talking about it. There are still WWII
vets who're reduced to shaking piles of weeping when they
try, for God's sake. And that's just the violence. You bottle
up the ways men cope with the tension, too. Booze. Porn.
Fights. Prostitutes. You're supposed to, anyhow—months
ago, Tillman confessed everything to Jen in a fit of honesty, dragging all their names across the soiled tableau of
his infidelities. She told Lish, so Desmond had to confess
a few things of his own. Too many things. "That's not
coping," Lish said. "That's just twisted." Now honesty is the
default. In theory.

The Kuwaiti pokes Desmond in the shoulder. "Am I
paying you to socialize or keep me safe?"

"Sorry, sir. Got some bad news is all."

"I don't care. Just drive and watch. Is that so difficult?"

"No, sir," Tillman and Desmond say at the same
time.

A creaky old water truck blocks the lane to the ministry
office, its Syrian driver squatting against one of the trailer's cracked, faded tires and chain smoking. The cab is
tilted forward, a strange balancing act, while the engine
disgorges a cloud of black smoke. Tillman radios the lead
vehicle to swing around to the other side of the block, but
a series of rare one-way streets foil the convoy's efforts to
get closer. Desmond growls into his radio to dismount.
Then Tillman takes the vehicles into their holding pattern, a laughable attempt at randomness to foil ambushes

—there are only so many ways you can vary the route when you can't be more than a minute away.

As they walk the Kuwaiti along the street, Desmond half expects Lish to call. His phone is on silent, but its buzzing against his leg—and she will try at least five times before giving up—would be a distraction. He walks right in front of the Kuwaiti, slightly to the side, while the other six men wedge through the pedestrians ahead and behind. Everything still glows softly, a gentle haze, but Lish's text has left an edge on his high like a metal burr you know you'll have to grind away at some point. When you can find the time. The will, maybe.

A noise out in front. One of the guys has manhandled an Indian man to a wall and is patting him down.

"Ease up," Desmond calls. "This isn't fucking Fallujah."

The Kuwaiti frowns. "That worker cannot say anything, and I would rather take no chances. Anyone could be a threat, yes?"

"Yes and no, sir," Desmond replies. "But it is better to be safe. Thank you."

Fuck. Bad impressions all around. The Indian man, skinny as a whip antenna, is just wearing a shirt and trousers, so the worst he could do is hide a pistol. His guy must be nervous to overreact so much after the initial scan. Here, on private duty when there are no armoured vehicles or tanks or swivelling fifty cals to push them aside, there's no way to avoid contact. You get so close to them here.

When they get inside the ministry, Desmond starts to guide the Kuwaiti towards the back of a queue forming in front of glassed-in cubicle. AC units against the wall do little against the heat and the temperature weight of hundreds of bodies, all foreigners with dark skin. Labourers, mostly, from the poorest countries, spending a long day away from their wages to move between lines, getting this signed, that stamped. The only sign in English hangs above the entrance, shouting, STATE OF KUWAIT. MINISTRY OF THE INTERIOR!

"No, no, we have to go upstairs," the Kuwaiti says. "To the offices."

"Our orders say you're filing paperwork," Desmond says.

"I am, but not down here. Not with *them*." He sniffs out the last word, his face pinching.

"Yes, sir."

"You come with me. Leave your men."

"Sir?"

"There's no room."

The stairwell is clad in polished stone, free of the dust and worn dullness characteristic of the ground floor. The hard surfaces sharpen the echoes from the din below, although the drug coursing its way through Desmond's bloodstream dulls the sounds. He is surprised, however, to hear his boots on each riser. *The fuck's that about?* he wonders. He certainly paid enough for the boots to expect a soundness ascent. Lish went shopping with him right after he signed the contract with the company, helping him wander through aisle after aisle of military and security gear in a store with no sign above the door. Word of mouth. Black plastic business cards with an address and a phone number. Army gear is all right, but the private stuff is heaven. Better fabrics, buckles, straps. Lighter. Higher ballistic protection. Still, even the best fabrics can't keep them from sweating in the heat or prevent salt-chafing. *Only the most expensive rashes for us*, he thinks, and has to stifle a giggle. The Kuwaiti frowns at him.

"What is so funny?"

"Nothing, sir. Dust in my throat."

At the third-floor landing, they pause for a few long moments while the Kuwaiti catches his breath. Eventually, they pass through a frosted door covered in Arabic numerals and script and into a large waiting area. Another surprise —the waiting area looks like it belongs in a palace. Rich woods, polished brass surfaces, deep sofas, silk carpets.

"Wait here," the Kuwaiti says.

He snaps a few sharp phrases at the receptionist, her aubergine *hijab* barely visible above the gleaming desk, before being buzzed through. Desmond moves to the side of the room where he can watch the entrance as well as the door through which his Primary has disappeared. Stands with his back against the wall. There is the smell of incense—bakhoor, the Kuwaitis call it—and something else just beyond his recall. Familiar, spicy. Desmond's vision begins to get hazy around the edges, his head feeling all at once as though it is turning a dozen times every second atop his neck yet is also detached from his body.

"Cardamom," he says, too loudly. "Jesus, that's the smell!"

"Are you all right, sir?"

The receptionist's hand reaches to her ear to activate the headset there. Desmond raises a hand to cut her off and keep her from calling. He walks to the desk, each step only a few inches but feeling like a mile, explaining that he's fine, that he'll be fine anyhow, if he can just have a moment. She stands, alarmed, and steps back from the desk and chair. Though the rest of her clothing is western in style, she is fully veiled by a black *niqab* draped across the lower part of her face. Her eyes are wide, panicked. And perfect, he thinks. Her eyes are perfect. Perfectly made up, subtle and dark. Symmetrical enough to fool their own mirror image. You'd declare an insurgency over them.

"What's your name?"

She tells him, her voice uncertain, but fucked if he doesn't forget it as soon as the name is spoken. God, those eyes. His mind is filled with the things he'd do to them, to her, twisted things without names, the sort you never say aloud. Is that his phone buzzing in his pocket somewhere off in the drug-induced distance? Must be Lish, reaching out about the travel delay, now an unwitting player in Desmond's fantasy.

Hold on, Troop, he tells himself. *Focus. The job. Straighten the fuck out.* He shakes his head and drags his eyes away from the woman, back to the entrance, scanning for threats. There is a detachment, though, a distance that he is having trouble passing over. All he needs is a suspect eleven-year-old to zero in the discipline, draw the sidearm, exit the grey matter that makes a person a person through the new cavern in the back of his skull. You don't wish for those things, but you wish for those things.

The Kuwaiti comes out from the offices, stops, and adjusts his igal and gutra. He has to be in his forties but his hands are as smooth as a child's, his nails precisely trimmed and buffed. The woman sits again in her chair and speaks to him in Arabic, some pleasantry. Deferent. The Kuwaiti dismisses her words with a grunt and walks out.

Desmond falls in, behind and slightly to the side, murmuring into the radio that the Primary is on the move. Tillman crackles a roger-that-we're-one-minute-out reply. Desmond knows what Tillman would say if he'd been in the reception area, too. *Bitch is smoking, Dez. Jesus. Did you see those fucking eyes?* Desmond would forgive the indiscretion, like always. Because those eyes. The kind of eyes you want to put a hollow-point through. Or that you want to lick. Depending.

DECLINATION

HASP KNEW THAT Angela, his mother's partner, couldn't wait to have him out of the house. His mother never said anything about what should happen after high school, and around her, Angela avoided the topic too. Privately it was a different story, albeit one without words. Today's permutation, a battered photo album full of drunken group shots and uncountable flipped-up thumbs stashed in his bedside drawer like strangely approved college porn. He'd woken to a muffled alarm, his phone having found its way into the drawer and set atop the album, just to make sure.

"I told you I don't have to decide until next year," he said, handing over the album when he came down for breakfast."

"Oh, my, where'd that end up?"

"Just stop, Angela."

"It's never too early to start looking for worms."

She smiled into her coffee and returned to her crossword. Hasp poured himself some cereal and milk and retreated to the dusty family room, shutting the window blinds against the morning sun and its too-bright radiator pattern on the wall. After a few minutes, he heard her yawn and stretch, accompanied by the clicks and rustles of getting ready for the day, her name tag clipped to the pen pocket of her teal blue scrubs, the once-over she always gave her med-kit. The grabbing of car keys like the chattering of glass teeth, the whisper of the door's weather stripping against the hallway floor.

He sat on the couch with his computer open on his lap. His morning routine—assuming his mother didn't call out for him—was to eat his cereal and then spend the remaining minutes before departure with his beloved online comics subscription. Sometimes the comics—left over from a recent breakup, an anniversary present from a girl he loved harder than you'd imagine—had to wait. Especially on the days his mother interrupted his solitude. Which was most days.

"Hasp! Hasp! Are you still here, baby?"

His mother's voice, perpetually breathless and reedy, wafted down the hallway that connected the living and sleeping parts of the small bungalow. He clapped the computer closed, slid it into his backpack, and went to his mother's room.

"'Morning, my love," she said.

"Hi, Mom."

There was a new smell in the air. A *wrong* smell.

He asked, "Did Angela stop in this morning?"

"Of course she did, baby. She always does."

"I smell something off."

"Oh, that must be my new perfume. Very expensive. Do you like it?"

"Very much, Mom."

"That's good—if you like it, Jack will too, I'm sure."

Hasp remained silent, used to the occasional confused references to her long-absent husband. He and Angela used to correct her, gently, of course, but that just made her agitated and irrational and made her heart rate spike. At first, there was a physical response to accompany the words, with waved arms and frantic rocking in the bed, but her arms were now too heavy and her torso lacked the internal strength to move hardly at all. Her neck still functioned, though, and she enjoyed turning to look out the window past the property line to where the deciduous trees clung to the rocky slope of the escarpment.

"A good day for a walk if I ever saw one," she said.

"I'll probably bike to school today."

"How are your ever going to get a girl if you don't get yourself a car?"

"Who has the time?" He held his breath, waiting for the crash of her displeasure. But the answer seemed to agree with her, and she nodded.

"Hard to buy a car when you're saving for college, I imagine."

"Sure, Mom."

He hadn't told her or Angela that there'd be no college or university, that he didn't really know what he was saving his money for. He worked part time at Pizza King, and his meagre pay accumulated slowly in his bank account. Angela took care of the bills, and her benefits covered the forest of medications in the bathroom cupboard.

He moved to the other side of the bed to draw the blinds—Angela usually opened them, blasting the room with morning light—and the smell worsened. He kept his face neutral as he reached behind her and lifted the edge of her gown, one of seven cotton shifts they could cover her with. This one was a faded blue-green, clean and smelling of lilies, but with frayed and stained edges.

"Oops, one of your pillows has fallen out," he said, lying.

"It's those synthetic ones Angela insists on," his mother says. "Too springy. Too light. Always falling out."

Here, the smell was stronger. He reached under one of the folds of skin and body fat and lifted it, turning away at the sight of the suppurating ulcers and the vinegary smell of fungal infection. Why hadn't Angela noticed and treated it?

"There," he said, laying the skin back in place. "That's much better, isn't it?"

She couldn't feel what he'd done, as though the nerve endings in her skin had stretched just too far. Angela would have to deal with it, he thought. She had a way of soothing his mother even in the face of medication—if he tried to apply any of the myriad ointments and creams, she always became agitated. Not Angela. Magic hands and voice, maybe.

"Much, much, much," she said. "I'm hungry."

He brought in a selection of cookies and muffins and potato chips and placed them on the hospital table that swung over the bed. She turned her face away from the large cup of water he offered and demanded fruit punch. When he brought some in, she sucked on the bright green straw like a baby, draining the cup quickly.

"More," she said, panting.

Hasp left another full cup next to the snack food, told

her that he didn't have time to hold this one for her but that Angela would help later, and went outside. He slung his pack over his shoulders and unlocked the bike from the rusted iron railings leading down from the front step. The house was set back a ways from the highway, mostly hidden by untended cedars that grew quickly on the low, wet parcel of land his father Jack had purchased before he left.

He tried to push away the thought of his mother dying. There was a new thinness to her breath, and the more frequent sores, and the things she said that seemed to hold less and less sanity. The other students were all thinking about next steps, college and university and things beyond, but he wasn't. The breakup had left him only with the subscription to that comics site, awkward night shifts at Pizza King, where he and Ginger had worked together, and an inability to deal with anything that had to do with school. Plus, an aching hole in his middle when he thinks about the baby her family made her take away when they moved, when he thinks about absent daddyhood. And thoughts about right now and an immediate future, about how shitty it would be to have to work full time and live at home, but how he couldn't really imagine it any other way, either. And the time to think about the day his mother would decide to give up, and how hard it would be for the emergency people to determine if there was or was not a heartbeat inside her. But the thought wouldn't leave, and he had to lean the bike back against the house to vomit onto the dirt in the house's shadow.

That's when the first precious thing appeared. It sat in the middle of his sick like a bright green eye, surrounded by an unmentionable stew yet perfectly clean. He picked it up, looked at it a long moment, and put it in his pocket—it felt odd, but had glittered so eagerly he couldn't resist.

He rolled his bike to the end of the driveway. Traffic was stalled along the highway. He pedalled hard along the soft shoulder, pleased at how quickly he passed all those stopped cars, and was already sweating by the time he reached the source of the backup a kilometre or so towards town. The red flares and the cherries atop the emergency vehicles danced across the scene. A jackknifed tractor trailer had slid across the median and taken out a minivan and a compact car. The first responders moved around everything in a sort of studied slow motion, as though there was nothing to hurry for.

❧

"How could you not see it? Smell it, for that matter?"

The argument had emerged over a dinner of leftover pizza from work. It wasn't going well, with Angela losing some of her measured calm when Hasp brought up the infection.

"I have to work. It takes time to care for her."

"You can't just ignore it!"

"Who's ignoring it?"

"It's at least a few days old."

"What the hell do you know about it?" Angela threw her slice back in the box and stood up quickly, rattling her glass of water a centimetre or so closer to the edge of the table.

"Jack! Angela! Stop arguing! It'll grow you old," his mother called from the bedroom.

"We're fine, Mom."

Angela called, "Do you need anything?"

"Pop! More pop!"

Angela fetched a two litre bottle of Coke from the fridge and walked out. Hasp tidied up the crusts and boxes and threw everything into the garbage. Later, after his mother fell asleep and Angela retired to her own room, Hasp laid in bed listening to the fading sound of late-night traffic on the highway. He dug into his jeans pocket and held the little green eye to the light of his bedside lamp. It was a button of some kind, with two small holes and a bevelled edge. He left it on the table and rolled over, thinking about the light that streamed through it.

Green fire, he thought, and fell asleep.

The next morning, Hasp surprised himself by waking before his alarm. It wasn't fully light outside yet. He didn't move for a good ten minutes, listening to the *Squeeeeee!* of the redwing blackbirds in the tall grass at the edge of their property, the green button clasped in one hand. He got up, dressed, put the button in his left front pocket, and went to the bathroom, amazed at how alert he felt despite getting an incomplete sleep.

When he went downstairs, he found Angela working at the kitchen table under a cone of overhead light, dressed only in boxers and an old shirt. Her head was leaned against her left hand as her right worked a silver laptop. Forms and pens were scattered around. She started when he came in, knocking an almost empty coffee mug to the floor, where it landed with a clunk, bouncing once, scattering a few dark droplets on the linoleum.

"Jesus!" she said.

"No, just me," he said. "Ha, ha."

She began gathering her things and rifling the papers into a loose pile. "You're up early."

"You, too. What's with the mess?"

"Here, let me get this stuff out of here, I have to—"

Hasp was about to tell her not to worry about it, that he'd eat on the couch like usual, when he saw the website open on the computer. Government logo. CANADA JOB BANK across the top.

"Thinking of a career change?" he asked.

"I'll tell you my business when you make it yours to pick a college."

"Is this what you've been doing instead of watching Mom?"

"You have no idea, kiddo. Just get your breakfast and go to school."

"Have you cleaned and dressed her sores yet?"

"Of course I have, just like every day."

"So how—"

"Damn it, I don't want to get into this again."

But the concern that had started as a niggling little thing had grown overnight, wedging itself behind his eyes while it was still small. Now it felt like a leaden tumour, the size of a golf ball, or perhaps a planet. He put the heel of his hand to his forehead and ground it in there, the pressure distracting him from his dizziness.

"Your fancy education didn't help with Mom's wound," he said.

He watched Angela's eyes fill as she sagged into the chair, aged by her slumped and rounded shoulders. "The wounds won't be getting better."

"But all the literature says that they're controllable and manageable—"

"*She* won't get better."

"But we've known that forever, right? That her weight gain might be permanent?"

Angela just stared at the edge of the kitchen table he'd eaten at all his life, with chrome edging and feet, the faux-wood surface worn through where elbows and forearms had rubbed and rubbed. And then he heard that detached voice again, hers this time, full of medical terminology but clarified by words like *immunological failure*, *metastasized*, *terminal*, *comfortable*. At the end, a long pause.

"Well," he said, "maybe now you'll lay off the university crap."

He turned away from her and reached for the bright yellow box in the cupboard. Have to buy some milk soon, he thought, assembling everything in a bowl, the last of the milk settling into the rice crisps with a satisfied crackling sound.

"Hasp—"

"No, really—a guy can finally get some peace," he said.

He plunged a spoon into the cereal and opened his mouth wide. Between the crunching of teeth and milk-induced popping, the kitchen was a pleasant blur of white noise. He'd never be able to say with any precision why the noise became so important on that morning, but it was. Maybe it was the filtering effect it had on Angela's words, like hearing too many would overwhelm him. As it was, when a few more words snuck through, between bites or in the middle of swallowing, they turned out to be overwhelming enough. *Lost my job. Weeks ago. Downsizing, etc. No benefits. Your mother's ... is expensive.*

Hasp dropped the bowl with a clatter to the scuffed Formica counter when a sudden abdominal spasm overtook him. He vomited cereal and milk all over the counter with such force that it practically bounced, spattering Angela's feet and the floor beyond. Hasp noticed a dark shiny object hit the floor and skitter past the lamp's pool of light, where it stopped in the gloom, glinting like an insect's tiny eye. He heaved again, but this time nothing came out, apart from a long, clingy string of mucus that clung to the first mess, suspended like some strange rope bridge between body and sickness.

Angela leaped to her feet. "Oh, come on—"

She was cut off by a sharp, panicked voice from down the hall.

"Angela! Jack! The light in here, it's—I'm hungry!—close the blinds, close the blinds!"

"Is that why she's not making much sense these days?" Hasp panted, wiping his mouth.

"Yeah, it's affecting her—"

"THIS ISN'T IT! TOO BRIGHT! TOO BRIGHT!"

Angela swore and moved towards the bedroom, leaving Hasp to lean against the counter and stare at the mess on the floor. But not for long—the little object's shine drew his eye even as he struggled to get his stomach's convulsions under control. He knelt and picked it up—like the green button, it was completely clean—and stared at it a long time. It was round and triangular all at once, like an almond, with uncountable facets that held the light a thousand different ways. But this one had black fire inside, deep and unexpectedly cool to the touch.

"You found them," the jeweller said with one raised eyebrow.

"I did," Hasp replied.

"Uh-huh."

The loupe wedged into the man's other eye fell to the end of its chain. He stood and stretched his back, muttering about how low tables and chairs would be the death of him yet. He'd come out of the workshop in the rear of the old store on Waterdown Road still wearing his worn apron and a multi-lensed apparatus tilted upwards from his face.

"Well, they're definitely good stones," he said. "Jadestone and black opal, I'd say, but you'd have to get that confirmed. Not something I do."

"Who does?"

"I can recommend a good appraiser, but it'll cost you."

"How much?"

"They charge by the hour. Two hundred per, if I recall."

Hasp bundled up the faded t-shirt scrap he'd made for the task. As he was about to stuff it in his pocket, the older man put his hand on Hasp's arm with a firm but not uncomfortable pressure. He looked hard at Hasp for a long moment before speaking. "I'm supposed to report this kind of thing, you know. The police are very interested in young men hawking rare gemstones."

"But I—"

"You said you found them, sure. And for some reason I believe you—maybe it's because you look sad rather than shifty."

Hasp took a deep breath. "Thank you."

"Be careful who you show those to—if they're the real thing, they're worth an awful lot."

Hasp thanked him again and walked out, accompanied by a soundtrack of cheerful bells hung above the door. The bells seemed to ring into his ears, down his neck, and into his stomach, where they blossomed into a now-familiar burning sensation. He lurched around the corner and just made it into the alley between the jeweller's store and the haberdashery next door. As he doubled over and again emptied the contents of his stomach onto the ground, this time a small dark sphere, marble-sized, tumbled out and into the mess. He knew this one even before he picked it up, its almost-mercury shine seeping through the dully reflective sheen.

"Black pearl," he said to the alley, wiping his mouth and digging for the scrap of shirt in his pocket.

❧

Hasp lost a few days with school and an unexpectedly long string of shifts at the Pizza King. Stan, the owner, had fired a few of the other workers in a fit of efficient streamlining. *You'll agree that it's fucking long overdue*, he'd said to Hasp a few nights before. Stan had to do the dough himself, a big job that meant he was around a lot, which meant a lot of time to say offensive things. *Those fuckers had it coming. Can you believe the fucking laziness these days? Didn't give a fuck, either, like they were entitled to our money.* Even though he was the sole owner, Stan liked to speak in the plural when he spoke about profits and costs.

A few days later, right after school and just before he was heading into work for yet another shift, Angela knocked on his bedroom door. She was dressed in jeans and a faded black polo shirt. Although she was pale and had dark circles under her eyes, he'd never seen her in fitted clothing before, had never noticed how fit and lean she was, the visible strength in her arms.

She caught his expression and chuckled. "Sometimes it's nice to feel off duty, even when you aren't, you know?"

He didn't respond.

"Can you stay home from school tomorrow morning? I have a job interview in Toronto."

"*You* want *me* to skip school? What about all those hopes and dreams—"

She held up her hands. "Can we call a truce? I'm too tired to argue."

"How long will you need?"

"Not long, but it's getting harder and harder to leave her alone. I'll make sure she's tended to before I go. You just have to stay nearby."

"I have a test in the afternoon," he said.

"I'll be back in time."

"All right."

"Thanks."

And she smiled at him, a bright, genuine smile, like new white paint on a highway. He nodded at her and noticed, just before closing his door again, a quiet in the house, as though its joints and mechanisms, and even the highway traffic out front, had paused for the moment of grace.

Much later that evening, he raised his head from the pages of the chapter he was supposed to learn for the quiz and wiped the drool from his chin. The side of his face that had lain against the page was warm, hot almost, and he worried that the ink might have transferred over. But on his way to the bathroom to check in the mirror, he was distracted by a cool breeze flowing in through a hallway window. Angela must have left it open, he thought, and he reached for the sliding panel and the short length of wood used to prop the window open. He stopped, his nose registering the distinct smell of marijuana sneaking in through the narrow space, faintly herbal, like it was being smoked a long ways upwind. Closing the window didn't cut it off completely, though. He walked down to the kitchen. Here, the smell was stronger, and lifted by soft, muffled laughter coming from down the hall.

Angela and his mother were together on the bed. The air was thick with the resinous smell of weed, the single lamp in the corner casting a yellowed hue through it like you'd see in a hotel from a 1970's movie. Their eyes were closed, and they didn't notice him come in or lean against the doorframe, stopped short by the sight of his mother's face, relaxed and worry-free for the first time in who knows how long. Angela was nestled close to his mother, a caring parenthesis against her side. There was a dark glass ashtray resting on his mother's stomach, the floral-printed fabric of her Thursday cover tight underneath. He stood there a while, watching both of them move with his mother's every breath, until he felt her eyes open and rest on him.

"Hi, baby. Need something?"

"Are you all right, Mom?"

"My, yes," she said, then nodded at Angela's resting form. "Been a long time since I got her into bed."

Angela stretched and sat up, swinging her legs to the floor. "Too long, my love."

"You'll be on top this time, right?"

His mother's words, spoken as though he wasn't there, sent both of them into another fit of giggles.

"Mom, come on. TMI," Hasp said, groaning.

Angela laughed, lifted the roach from the ashtray, and flamed it back into life before passing it to his mother, who drew long and deep before offering it to him. He often smoked up behind the Pizza King after Stan went home—at least he had until Stan fired most of his staff—but now he declined.

His mother shrugged, the whole bed shifting from the movement. "Your loss, baby."

"What's going on? What's with the weed?"

"Angela says it's good for cases like mine. What did you call it, my love? Pain management?"

"But you need to—"

"Especially for terminal cases like mine. It worked too —I don't feel a thing. Straightened me right the fuck out," she said, and inhaled again. Held it. Exhaled. Another giggle.

His mother swearing—he hadn't heard it for a long

time. Since before spiritual conversions marked on old calendars, promises to deities and life to make it right, change, straighten everything out. Absorbed in assembling another joint from all the gear on the night-table, Angela didn't notice the look. His mother did, though.

"She told me, Hasp. Although I already knew, in a way."

"I'm just—I don't know—"

"Worry will make you old, sweetie. There's no future in it."

"How could I not worry?"

"I know this is heavy, but you need to try. You need to—you've been so down the past while."

"I'm fine."

"I know that girl's gone. I could trace it to the day—it's all over your face."

Angela, studiously engaged in perfecting her roll and seal, remained silent. Knowingly so.

He took a step into the room, closer to the bed, and tried to look her in the eye so he could begin—these are not conversations to be had obliquely. But as he drew near, her eyes started darting back and forth and her face grew florid. Angela sighed, dropped the unlit joint into the ashtray, moved it to the bedside table, and brushed her hands free of the dregs that stuck there like bits of oregano. His mother's movements became more frantic, shifting the floorboards, the room, the house. An entire life, maybe.

"No, no, NO! I'm wearing far too much—TOO HOT, TOO HOT!"

"Wendolyn, darling, I'm here. What do you need?"

"WE CAN TAKE THAT TRIP, JACKIE BABY! 'Round the world, you said, right?"

Angela looked at him as she rubbed his mother's arm. "We lost her again," she said.

"For how long?"

She shrugged and leaned in closer to his mother's ear, speaking in such a low voice Hasp couldn't hear what was being said. He could hear the tone, though, calm and murmuring. His mother tried to shake Angela free, dropped her chin to her heaving chest, and began rubbing her own girth with both hands, around and around. Angela held on and kept whispering.

"We'll cross the equator, Jack. LONGITUDE! LATITUDE! COMPASS POINTS! DECLINATION! I learned them right, didn't I? You said I had to."

And then his mother fell silent, her eyes closing. Hasp had been moved back to the wall by the first stormy blasts of her outburst—the cool of the plaster was quick to seep through his thin shirt, making him dizzy and his vision fade. This time when he vomited, the precious object was clearly a diamond, large and smoky and crystalline and uncountably faceted.

Angela spoke without looking up. "Look at the mess you've made. Get on your knees and clean it up—I can't do everything, you know."

The offer was way too low, he knew, but it was still an enormous amount of money. The pawn broker, a fat man stretching the seams of an old Air Jordan track suit but shining like Midas around the neck and at the first phalange of every finger, sat back and folded his arms. He

watched Hasp from behind the thick Plexiglas that protected his back room and the bulk of his displayed jewellery. The rest of the store was filled with more prosaic
things—clothing, sports equipment, dated electronics—
the necessary cast-offs of need. He had no doubt that the
lazy old bastard had undercut those offers, too, but there's
little negotiating room from the starting point of despera-
tion. And those poor souls weren't pawning exquisite gemstones, either.

"I'll take it," he said.

The man got up from his stool with a sluggish grunt
and disappeared into the back. He'd had the honesty, at
least, to leave the diamond on the worn patch of black
velvet he'd brought out for the transaction. Hasp had decided to try and sell the diamond first, being the most
easily appraised and recognizable, and had already learned
two valuable things—first, the stone was worth far more
than he could have guessed, and two, never tell a pawn-
broker you'll think about the offer and get back to him.
At the last place, a musty hovel on King Street in
Hamilton, the guy behind the desk had hemmed and
hawed, talking about Canada Revenue Agency limits on
cash transactions and needing some time to put the
money together. Hasp hadn't thought too much about it
until he returned a short while later to find an old Monte
Carlo parked in front of the pawnshop with two huge
men inside smoking and watching the door. If the stone
was worth enough to wave away the risk of a daylight rob-
bery two blocks from the central police station, it was
better to get out of town and plan a little bit better. Hasp
was able to walk away unnoticed and then, when the

jitters hit, duck behind a dumpster and be sick. There was another diamond to recover, this one a subtle pink and roughly the same size as the first. Which gave him the courage to skip school and make his way to this Toronto pawn shop on Bloor West at the end of the subway line.

"It's a lot of cash," Fat Air Jordan said when he eased himself back onto the stool. "Let me call you a cab so you're not walking around."

He laid out the stacks of bills, each stack surprisingly thin and tight because of the polymer, and pushed them over. As soon as Hasp touched the first bundle—pushing a renegade upswell of hope back down—and stuffed it into the padded mailer envelope he'd brought along, the diamond disappeared.

"No, thanks. I'm okay."

He walked to the cab he'd left waiting a few doors down, got out at Old Mill station, took the train a few stops, walked up to a post office at street level, mailed the padded envelope to himself in Waterdown, got back on the train and repeated the process three more times at various places around the city. He vomited as many times, too, stumbling out of the post offices and managing to find quiet spaces in time. Just before boarding the GO train back to Aldershot, he sat down for a burger and fries at a pub just outside Union Station. It was there that he let himself get excited about what Monday's mail would bring. About whether a cure for his mother's cancer could be found in bundles of money. About paying for his meal with a slippery twenty-dollar-bill. About the weight of the change he'd receive, and whether he'd notice it on the ride home.

Any doubt he felt about the path he'd chosen was erased the moment he arrived back home. He didn't think much about the OPP cruiser at the end of the driveway, at least not at first, assuming that the officer bent over paperwork under the jaundiced dome light was setting up a speed trap. But there were also new ruts in the soft ground next to the driveway, deep and double-wheeled, the disturbed ground already filling with muddy water, the soil almost black. Dozens of muddy boot prints tracked up the steps and straight through the kitchen, where Angela sat at the table, head on her arms.

"Hasp, you're here," she said.

No kidding, he wanted to say. But then it occurred to him that Angela didn't usually waste her breath on such banalities, that these were the words of a person at a loss for many more.

"What happened?"

"They laughed at her when they were planning how to load her up," she said. "The guy said, *What are we, fucking mechanics?* Then they laughed about another call they'd been to, about having to knock down a wall but forgetting to take down the artwork first."

Hasp left her at the table and followed the muddy footpath to his mother's room. There was enough light from the evening sun through her curtains to see the tracks surrounding the bed but concentrated on the far side under the window, how thoroughly the mud had saturated the carpet. She looked as she always did in the grip of her fitful version of sleep, the covers hitching and falling, her laboured breathing almost a physical presence. There was a brief, heady urge to throw the light switch and soak the room in light so he could inspect her properly. Angela's whispered voice surprised a momentary choking sound from his suddenly constricted throat, and he hurriedly closed the door, lest his mother's rest be disturbed.

"I'm ninety percent sure there are internal injuries, but she refused transport to the hospital."

"How? From what?"

"She fell out of the bed. Got herself wedged between the bed and the wall."

"When—"

"I was out grabbing some groceries—the cupboards were bare—but it took longer than I thought—"

"You weren't here?"

"I found her when I got back and called 911."

"And—?"

Angela held a finger to her lips. "Let's go back to the kitchen, okay? She just went down a few minutes before you got home."

"Is she going to be all right?"

But Angela wouldn't say anything until they sat in opposite chairs. This side of the house didn't get the sunset at all, so the room was dark, apart from the hanging lamp over the table. The harsh light, straight down, hollowed out her cheeks and left her eyes in shadow, a skeleton recounting a near-death tale, one where the main character was a forty-something obese woman who tried to get out of bed and ended up pressed against the wall, cutting off her own breath and circulation. Where it took two EMTs and an OPP officer to hold her up enough to breathe until the fire service rescue squad arrived some fifteen minutes later. How they talked about cutting through the wall until she refused to be transported anywhere, how the rescue guys had to assemble a special hoist right in the room to lift her back into her bed. How Angela begged for her to be taken to the hospital, how his mom refused, saying she'd prefer to die at home and with some dignity.

Die with dignity. That was the phrase Ginger used to describe why they'd stayed in Waterdown so long, just before she left with the baby. *Grandpapa wanted to die with dignity. Here. Where he made a life.* When he died, she and her parents simply sold everything and left.

"This doesn't feel very dignified," Hasp said.

"No, it doesn't. And if she doesn't want to—can't—fight, what's the point?"

"You'll find work. It'll help."

"Doesn't matter—benefits nowadays don't cover the kinds of treatments she'll need in the time she has left."

His phone trilled loudly from his pocket just as he was about to tell her to wait until Monday, when he'd take care of everything. He took it out and looked at the screen. Pizza King. Stan was already yelling obscenities when he tapped the green button and accepted the call, first threatening to fire him for missing his Friday night shift, then backtracking and saying how valued Hasp was and begging him to come in. Hasp hung up on him without a word, allowing the tiniest sliver of satisfaction to slip in between his and Angela's heartbreak, so he could tell her his plan. But she had already gotten up to head back into his mother's bedroom, silently apart from the dusty scrape of her slippers moving along the soiled hallway.

On Monday, the temperature and humidity spiked to the mid-thirties. Everything seemed to move in slow motion, even the cars along the highway and the airplanes streaking white far above the groundborne blanketing haze. Even water from the tap produced an opaque screen of condensation on the glass a few seconds after being poured. His loosest jeans and t-shirt still felt too close, itchy.

His grand presentation had to wait an extra hour. The rural mail delivery car had made its delivery at the usual time but left only the usual smattering of bills and ad-mail and a small, barcoded parcel notification card. Of course, he'd thought, stuffing the card in his pocket behind his wallet, the envelopes wouldn't have fit in the oblong mailbox at the end of the driveway. So much for a perfect plan. He'd pedalled hard enough into town that he was sweating by the time he locked up his bike outside the drug store and walked to the to the post office kiosk at the back, next to the pharmacy. The clerk scanned the card and his ID and handed over the bubble mailers in a single, teetering pile. A dirty pile, too, grimy even from a three-day journey across fewer than a hundred kilometres.

Angela wrinkled her nose when he came in, his shirt soaking wet on his back where the pack had sat, rushed past her and went up the stairs. He opened the mailers on his bed and allowed the bundles to form into a sprawling pile. It wouldn't have been enough to say it was the most money he'd ever seen—it was, in fact, far more than he could ever have pictured, much less belonging to him and resting on his bed.

A few minutes later, having cooled down enough to be presentable, he put the bills in a cloth grocery bag and went downstairs. Angela had brought her supply of weed into the bedroom again, and they were smiling at each other and laughing quietly. His mother saw him, and her glassy eyes brightened, before filling with tears at an uneven and violent sequence of coughs that rattled wetly from somewhere deep inside. When they finally subsided, she seemed to deflate into the bed and become even paler, like once-bright canvas bleached in the sun. He looked at Angela, who'd sat back to give his mother room and regarded her with concern. Neither seemed to notice the bag.

"Hi, baby," his mother said.

"How're you feeling, Mom?"

"Oh, something happened to my lungs the other day. They feel bruised and all full of holes."

"I told you today would be difficult," Angela said, wiping her forehead with a wet cloth. "The humidity is murdering the air quality."

"It's *not* the humidity, my love. You know that."

Angela sighed and passed over the joint. His mother drew deeply and held it until another bout of coughing overtook her. Hasp noticed new blotches of deep colour on her shins and calves, as well as on a swell of body fat that pressed out of a gap between cover and bed sheet. It had been a difficult weekend in many ways. Her regular periods of dementia had become uneven and unpredictable, from deep depressive sessions of weeping to screamed obscenities at both him and Angela to calm periods of disoriented reflection. He'd gone in to sling dough at the Pizza

King, mostly to do something mindless and get away from the stuffy house. And the waiting. He'd thought about telling them about the money a few times, but backed away each time.

"You should bring your girl over for dinner again, sweetie—Ginger, is it? I like her," his mother said, smiling out the window at the escarpment beyond.

He traded a look with Angela, who took the joint from his mother's fingers and stubbed it out on the ashtray.

"Mom, Angela, I have some good news."

"Oh? That's nice, Hasp. But get Jack in here, too—he could use some good news. *He can't afford the boat he wants us to take out. He's pretty upset*," she said in a stage whisper.

"What is it?" Angela asked.

He unslung the bag, brought it over to the bed, and gently dumped the money on the flat sheets between his mother's splayed legs. The gemstones skittered here and there—the stress of the weekend had added to the haul. Angela's sharp intake of breath was quick and loud in the room.

"Jesus, Hasp. That has to be, like—" Angela said, looking for a number. "And those stones—"

"That looks like plastic funny money," his mother said, and giggled.

"Where did you—"

"We can pay for Mom's care now. She's refused all the government help. We could put her somewhere private and get her the help she needs."

"Jack? Did you rob a bank?" his mother asked, her face getting red.

"Shhhhh, Wendolyn," Angela said.

"Because if you did something dirty to get that, I'd never forgive you."

"No, I earned it—it's all legal."

"How?" Angela asked. "There's no way."

"I just did."

"Get it away from me, Jack. You promised we'd save up and not do anything drastic. I can't believe you'd—YOU PROMISED!"

"You better go—I don't want her too get worked up right now," Angela said, grabbing the bundles and pinching up the stones into the bag, pushing it hard against his chest.

"All this silly new talk I can't get my head around—TACK! JIB! PERMISSION TO COME ABOARD! NOTHING BUT GLASS OUT THERE MOST DAYS!"

Angela took his arm and led him out, closing the door behind them. His mother's voice beat against the inside of the door with the weak fury of an infant's hands. The sound faded as Angela led him back into the kitchen.

"I'm sorry," she said. "This is all my fault."

"What? Not at all—I want to help pay—"

"Hasp, no. I don't know where that money came from, how you got it, or whether it's possible to give it back, but you have to take it away."

"I'm not in any trouble."

"I want it out of the house."

"I can't just deposit it into a bank—"

"Maybe I was too aggressive with all the university stuff."

"—but we can pay for things as they come up."

"She's going to die, Hasp—you should be getting ready for that."

"I just wanted to help."

"You should be thinking about what will happen afterwards, too."

"Like what?"

Angela just breathed deeply, patted his shoulder, and went back to his mother's room. He stood in the kitchen for a long while before heading upstairs. In his room, he tossed the bag onto his bed and sat next to it. He removed all the bills and stones and organized them into neat piles, counting, planning, denying. He spent the rest of the day in and out of the bathroom, forcing his fingers down his throat and dry-heaving into the empty toilet, barely rippling the surface of the water there.

BARTON WALKUP

"A THOUSAND BUCKS is still a thousand bucks," Vik says.

"But it's not about the money," I say.

"It's always about the money, Gail."

I turn back to the stove, where my water has begun to boil. I add my spices. Four cloves. One cinnamon stick. Four pods of green cardamom, each bruised with a bite. The rolling water tumbles the spices over and around each other.

I ask, "Will you tell Francesca?"

"No. But does this change things for you? As in—" He waves his hands around as if to say, All of this?

"I don't know," I say. "Probably not."

My mother sent the package general delivery. In a weak moment a few weeks ago I called home and she got it out of me that I'm living in Hamilton with friends I met in India. Her first question: How are you for money? It's always her first question. She told me she'd send something, so I've been passing the post office every day since. It arrived yesterday. Inside the crumpled bubble-mailer an open-ended airline ticket to Brussels and a Visa card pre-loaded with a thousand US dollars.

Vik shakes his head. "A paper airline ticket," he says. "Didn't know they were still an option."

"Harder to say no when it's actually in your hands," I say.

I remove the pot and pour in a measure of loose Assam tea. Stir it all together. Vik and I stand next to each other in silence as the tea steeps. I place the pot back on the burner. Medium heat. Reach for the milk and pour it in until the chai becomes just the right shade. Add sugar. Stir the chai as it warms, the heat moving the tea around in seemingly random directions.

You have to use whole milk. Vik, an engineer by trade, always goes right to the chemistry of it, saying how the masala is made up of aromatic spices best released in alcohols or fats. Something about a benzene ring. But I'm not so scientific. I just rely on the recipe given to me at a railway kiosk in Delhi by a tiny man surrounded by scorched pots, burners, and stacks of paper cups. His shirt and trousers were always pressed and clean, despite the ever-present mess and bustle.

"Smell that reaction," Vik says, leaning over the pot.

"You're such a fucking geek," I say.

"I am indeed a fucking geek, and you love it."

He tries to throw a sly smile over his shoulder as he leaves the kitchen, but I drag him back and plant a kiss right on his smooth cheek. Gay Indian guys take smooth skin to a new level.

I get these little crushes on unlikely men. I know there's no chance with any of them, but I don't buy the theory that says a person's love is finite, that some gets chipped away with each attempt. I crushed on the Delhi chai wallah, too. I couldn't say how old he was, but was taken in by his lonely manner, his surprisingly good English, and those clean, pressed clothes. He gave me his recipe. Most of it. "I am keeping one ingredient to myself, Miss," he said. "Or no one is buying my tea and they are buying yours." He did that amazing cooling pour, the two paper cups three feet apart and without a single spilled drop. I smiled and accepted the chai with a free hand. I took a sip. Faint liquorice. I said it was star anise. "No, Miss. It is a secret and I will never tell." But I could see he was pleased. I don't use the anise, as it tends to take over.

"Chai in five minutes," I call into the living room.

"Thanks, chai wallah Gail!" comes the chanted response.

Like they've been rehearsing. Francesca's always organizing us into tasks and order—*Let's march sometime! Let's all paint our names above the door!*—like it's subconscious, or built in. She calls us The Collective. Burning all of our identification was her idea. *How else are we supposed to truly live free?*

My father was a diplomat, so we were posted all over the world. I was born and cut my teeth in Colombo, strung my first sentences together in Dhaka, got my first kiss in Moscow, reached puberty in Delhi, and graduated from high school in Seoul. I went back to Delhi between second and third year at university and discovered the truth about chai. I learned, too, that Indians still marvelled at tall, redheaded girls, especially ones travelling on their own.

I pour the chai into small, clear teacups I picked up at the Sally Ann on King Street, load them onto a tray, and walk into the main room.

Vik winks at me when he takes his tea and raises his glass. "To the chemistry of it," he says.

"Ha, ha," I say.

Francesca leans forward. "And now to business—"

"First things first," Vik says, cutting her off. "Stuart? I think you have something for us?"

Stuart pulls out an eighth and some papers. We sip and smoke in silence for a little while.

Francesca asks, "Ever think about going back again?"

No one answers. She asks the question at least once a week, even though none of us can afford to go. We've been living in the little Barton Street walkup for a couple of years, refusing full time work and working only for cash. The question usually comes out when she's high on weed, so we're able to deflect smoothly, laughingly, most of the time. This time we just sip our chai and lean back on the cushions with our eyes closed—sometimes uncomfortable conversations can just waft away like vapour.

"You got good stuff this time," Vik says, nodding at Stuart.

"The best," I say.

"Glad you like it."

I ask if he'll stick around for a bit. Stuart scratches a scab on his arm, small, like you get when you attack a mosquito bite too vigorously, and shakes his head. "Places to be, and all that. It's good chai, Gail."

"Thanks."

Stuart was the only one who went back to heroin after Delhi. India had a way of sneaking between my layers, so after university I stuffed a few things in a pack and went back. I preferred to travel alone but the need for affordable lodging brought us to the same hostel, one used to westerners staying long term. Finding themselves. Vik, Francesca, and I blame the quality of the cut, that we scored some really bad smack, even though there was no way for us to know and it felt pure enough at the time. We chased it according to the dealer's instructions and the high was balloons and soaring dreams, just like everyone said. But it made me feel like hell afterward so I never touched it again. Nor did Francesca or Vik, but Stuart couldn't stay away. Can't.

"Before you go, let's talk business," Francesca declares. "Stuart?"

"Nothing. Just the weed."

"Vik?"

"Nada."

"Gail?"

I reach into my pocket for a couple of damp twenties, a five, and some loonies. Lay it all on the serving tray in the centre of the living room floor we use as our coffee table. Ignore the extra looks Vik is throwing my way—maybe I shouldn't have told him about Mom's package. I'm good with numbers, so one of the shops up James North pays me cash to go through their receipts and invoices every so often. Francesca studiously ignores the contradiction between the tired but dressy outfit I wear for my numbers work and our usual thrift-store couture. We don't even have cellphones—she is, of course, anti-technology—so looking for work is old school, door to door, handshakes, promises.

Francesca scoops up the money and walks over to the heat register where we keep the stash. I'm the numbers person, but she takes care of the money, like everything else. The grate scrapes free and she pulls out the small box with brass hinges and inlaid mother-of-pearl. A thirteenth birthday gift from my mother. Hand-carved, Goan mahogany, it protected my meagre supply of jewellery all the way through university. It was snatched up by Francesca the moment she saw it. "You don't mind, do you? It's for The Collective." It's the only piece of my former life as a foreign service brat I've carried into adulthood, aside from all those travel memories, snippets of languages, and the guilty sense of superiority we feel when we talk to people who've never travelled.

"Will you be back tonight?" Francesca asks Stuart, who's already levering himself into his coat, a knee-length army surplus parka.

He used to fill that thing, I think, as he shrugs, his whole frame moving rather than just his shoulders. As he throws the baggie with the leftover weed onto the tray, I have the urge to force him back onto the cushions and wrap him in myself until he falls asleep.

"I don't know. We'll see," he says.

"This is home. You should come home," Francesca says to his back as he slips out into the February cold.

Sal lets himself in at seven the next morning.

I'm up early to a breakfast of muesli and coffee and a dog-eared novel. He nudges Francesca awake with his foot. She flinches into a sitting position, squinting, no doubt ready to let fly a cutting remark.

"Well, good morning to you too," she says, recognizing him.

He doesn't reply and moves towards the empty room at the back of the apartment.

Francesca yawns and swishes some water around her mouth from the glass next to her bedroll. She looks over to Stuart's corner where his bedroll is still bound and leaning against the wall before getting up and following Sal. The door to the back room closes with a click. Vik stirs, mumbling something in his sleep, before falling silent again.

Sal is the owner of the building and lets us stay as long as Francesca keeps his penis happy. There was a rental sign in the upstairs window, but when Sal met Francesca, the deal shifted. He stopped taking our rent, hinted with looks and innuendos. She just shrugged, said it was all for The Collective. For Sal, it's nothing but win-win. The store below is vacant, its windows soaped and papered. The city gives tax breaks for vacant storefronts in depressed neighbourhoods. Sal's other properties are leveraged in, so he actually makes money by leaving the Barton property alone. Occasionally, he'll use the space for a few days at a time, with a lot of guys coming and going at odd hours. He never visits Francesca during those times. Our bedrolls and sleeping bags remain like a strange camping exhibit in the large main room. No furniture at all. The back room has a new single bed, velvet curtains, and even an antique rolltop writing desk. We aren't allowed back there. Only Francesca is. Only when Sal comes for his ritual servicing.

She comes out a short while later, arranging her clothing and looking weary.

I ask, "Did he go down all right?" It's out before I can stop myself. Sarcastic, like Sal's a sleeping infant.

"Fuck you."

She doesn't say it with any malice, really, just a tone so flat you'd lean it towards contempt. She yawns and pours herself the last of the coffee from the French press, as chilled as the apartment floor, but doesn't offer to make more.

I never know how to respond to Francesca's way of paying the rent. It disgusts me, yet she's quick to use her body to get things. It certainly saves us a lot, and Sal has someone around to fuck and keep an eye on his property, all for free. I get up and go to the sink to wash my dishes and a few others that have piled up. The water is cold enough to make my hands ache.

Vik comes in, groggily scratching himself. "What's for breakfast?"

"Me," I say, hoping my voice sounds light as I nod at the bulge in the thin track pants he sleeps in.

He follows my gaze. "Morning wood," he says and laughs, thrusting his hips forward and his shoulders back.

He takes a few jaunty steps around the kitchen as though the sight of his substantial erection is nothing to get all sticky and warm about. I plunge my hands back into the frigid suds to keep me from thinking any more about fucking him straight. Hold them there as penance for being ridiculous.

"Charming," Francesca says from the other room.

"So, what are you lovely ladies up to today?"

Francesca walks in and drops her dishes in my water.

"O'Doyle's might need some extra servers for tonight. We could use some extra cash. Gail? How about it?"

A few months ago, we helped out with a stag party, the owner paying us under the table. Francesca is looking expectantly at me and dragging a bamboo comb through her tatted, mousy hair. The movement is harsh but she almost seems to relish it.

"No, thanks," I say. "I'm going to get centred."

A ridiculous statement, but camouflage enough. Francesca nods and faces Vikram. "What about you?"

"Nope. Family thing up the mountain."

Francesca and I make noises of surprise. We don't do family things. The whole point is to cut off the world and its attachments, including the risk of family generosity. *Live real*, as Francesca says. At first, it seemed easy to take our little vow to live only on what we could find. Vik, Stuart, and I sucked it up, pulled along by our loyalty to Francesca and the wistful memory of the dynamic self-denial she championed in Delhi. In that place, it seemed effortless for her to lead, for us to follow. It took so little to survive. Thrive, even. When we moved to Hamilton, we knew it would be different, but still promised each other that we'd never beg or knock on charity doors. Convincing ourselves that dumpster-diving wasn't like begging. After a few months, though, even Francesca had reached her limit. "All right, but only cash jobs, nothing regular," she said. Vik, content to work and live day to day like the rest of us, rarely talks about his family.

"My baby sister's getting married today," he says. "They've been celebrating all week."

Francesca sucks her teeth in reproach. Before she can

launch into a sermon, I ask if he'd even be allowed to attend. Vik's conservative parents stopped talking to him when he came out years ago. Like me, he was in India finding himself—like me, he stood out, his effeminate mannerisms as stark against the Indian social scene as my freckles and fiery hair.

"I guess I'll find out," he says.

"I didn't know you were still in contact," I say.

"Just with my sisters."

"You said that living here wouldn't be an issue," Francesca says.

Vik shrugs. He's the only Hamiltonian in our little foursome. When he got back from India, he vanished into the Toronto queer scene. Francesca returned to whatever kept her occupied out west. I became your typical rootless repatriate, eking out a living as a bookkeeper here and there. After a while, we all felt a tug and began emailing and chatting about living together again, keeping alive that dream of simplicity. Vik mentioned the Barton neighbourhood as a possibility: rusted fire-escapes, layered gang-tags in every alley, daylight prostitutes, lots of dodgy but cheap accommodation, a brand of anonymity you find only in the poorest areas of mid-sized cities. We jumped at the idea. Somehow, Hamilton seemed safe. Removed. Even Stuart, living with his disappointed parents, his meagre earnings having nowhere else to go other than his veins, liked the idea.

I ask, "Want me to come along?"

Vik laughs and gives me a hug from behind. God, his chest and arms are warm. Plunge, scrub, rinse.

"Thanks, but showing up with a tall ginger goddess might make it hard to blend in."

"You're a brown racist," I say.

"You love it, chai wallah."

"They're going to see you anyway."

"Yeah, I know."

"Maybe you can sneak some food back for us later."

"I'll eat it all myself. God, I miss the food."

He sighs, releases me—I almost fall backwards—and goes back to his cereal.

I fell in love with Vik at that dingy hostel in Old Delhi. Perhaps love's the wrong word, but it didn't seem to matter. Even a fling with Stuart didn't phase Vik. I was a bad sitcom cliché, but that didn't change anything. I did my best to get away from the hostel on temple trips and sightseeing jaunts, but my longing fit easily into my old surplus backpack.

I close my novel, stretch, and look at the clock. I just lost an hour or so. Vik's gone, as is Francesca, who said she was heading out to O'Doyle's but I know she's really out looking for Stuart. The apartment feels too empty, so I smoke a pinner for company and herbal calm. I'm planning a guerrilla run to the fourth floor of the central library, where I can disappear behind one of the public access computers. Francesca would flip if she knew, but I log in about once a month, afraid more of losing access to my online accounts than I am of her piousness. I get up, roll up my sleeping bag, douse the roach in the sink, and walk over to the coat hooks by the door.

Sal comes out of the room, his eyes puffy from sleep. He's ugly and gorgeous all at once, his blotchy complexion and butcher's hands locked in a perpetual argument with his impeccable clothes and showroom body. He looks around.

"Francesca's gone," I say.

"I see that. I need to talk to her—when's she back?"

"I have no idea."

"Where are you going?"

"Out."

"Out where?"

"Just out."

He frowns, looking for an instant like he wants to get more into it but instead puts on his coat. "I meant to give her a message earlier, but I fell asleep," he says.

I wait.

"It affects you too."

I still wait.

"Your buddy's been stealing things from some of our people to pay for his habit. "

"So?"

"Francesca's a friend, so I'll give him one chance to stop. If he can't, this apartment goes away for all of you, and he becomes like anyone who steals from us."

He draws the last word out to give it some extra weight, but it seems rather comical to me. "What, you're not the boss?"

He glares at me and, without another word, walks out, leaving both doors—the apartment and the outside door at the bottom of the stairs—open to the wind, which rushes up the stairs three or four at a time. It isn't a message you leave on a scrap of paper taped to the fridge. Maybe I'll find Francesca on the way. Ordinarily, I walk up Barton and then south on James to get to the library, but I decide to zig-zag down and through the grid of side streets, a better recipe for finding someone looking for someone else who doesn't want to be found.

It's been more than a week since Stuart left. Sal's only taken Francesca into the back room once and left right after he was finished. She came out and said he'd threatened us again because Stuart was still stealing things. "Which means he's still alive," she said. She's lost some weight since Stuart left, her wraps and frayed jeans starting to hang on her already thin frame. Vik has been quiet since the wedding. Although he and I have both found some work this week and there's enough in the stash box for a few grocery runs, Francesca's worry is infecting us too. We catch each other covering plates of food with foil and leaving them in the fridge but don't talk about it. Chai is a welcome distraction even as our collective concern takes something away from sharing its warmth.

"It tastes different," Vik says, frowning at his teacup.

"It's the same," I say.

"No, I taste it too," Francesca says.

"Should I stop making it?"

No, they say in quiet unison, although she's looking at her cup rather than drinking, and he already has his new cellphone out. His parents made a scene at the wedding. He left, but his other sister chased him down and gave him some cash and her number, made him promise to buy a mobile. In the phone's blue glow, his eyes are black spots on his face but his smile is bright. Francesca looks at him and sighs but has given up on her technology rebukes. A moment later, she begins pacing the room but catches herself before her third turn, slapping her hand hard against the doorframe between the open room and the kitchen before dumping her tea in the sink.

"Fuck. I'm going out," she says.

"He'll come back when he's ready," Vik says without looking up from the phone.

"You keep saying that, like you have some magic formula for how people are," she says.

He turns off the phone's screen and shakes his head. "No magic recipe. Not people. Just Stuart."

Francesca turns to me. "I'm supposed to do groceries today," she says. "Can you do it? Take whatever cash you need from the stash."

In my peripheral vision, I catch Vik's shocked look, but I hold her gaze.

"Sure," I say.

She leaves, not quite closing the door. Cool air whispers through the dark gap until Vik closes it behind her. "Wow. She never lets anyone handle the stash," he says.

"Especially me."

"Have you told her about your Mom's package?"

"No. Do you think she'd be able to resist talking about it?"

"Probably not. But—"

"She'd act all betrayed, like I let her down."

"Well, you could give it to The Collective."

"Fuck off, Vik. Even you can't say the name without cringing."

"And you can?"

"None of us can. Except her."

I collect the three teacups and remnant chai, dumping each cup into the sink. I empty the pot next, sieve the leaves and spices and knock them into the garbage. Vick follows me into the kitchen and leans against the fridge.

"I want to talk to her," he says. "About Stuart, I mean —it's eating her up."

"Yeah."

"Can you do it? Maybe a female perspective—"

"No. She wouldn't hear it from me. When it comes to Stuart—"

"Everyone is a threat, I know."

Stuart still hates it when I describe our night together in Delhi as a fling. I never admitted that I was using him to get Vik's attention, but was as direct as I could be. "It's not that it was nothing," I said in the hostel's common area, "but fate didn't bring us together to become attached that way." Two weeks later, I walked into the dorm room we all shared and found Stuart and Francesca having sex—a week after that they pushed the rusty old hospital beds together. She got defensive when Vik and I ribbed her about it. "Don't you dare call it making love," she snapped. "We're just fucking. It's an animal need." But she couldn't compete with Stuart's love affair with dirty Delhi smack, and it ended. They never got back together but she's not over him, either. Parallel waste. Her love, his life.

Eventually, as our visas neared their expiry dates, we made promises to reconnect someday and went our separate ways. Wispy things, those kinds of promises, yet enough to bring us to Barton Street in a city only one of us knows.

"She'll come around," Vik says.

"I hope so."

His phone rings, an alien sound in our small space. He mumbles an excuse and walks through to the common room. The wedding has changed him; he's pulling away. I've been wanting to ask for more details all week but feel strange about it, making my chai and reading my novels rather than speaking just in case his words make me want to pull away too. Pull away sooner, that is. Those tempting library computers are doorways to applications, accounts, connections. Secret stories. We all have them. At first Vik told us his parents were dead, only later admitting that it isn't true, that it's just easier to call them dead than explain the fractures he suffered in being cast out from his family. Aside from the few dollars his sister gave him, he has no money. He actually followed Francesca's directive and gave away the significant cash he'd made filming gay porn for the Indian black market. But he'll always have plenty of options. Beautiful men with few inhibitions generally do.

After grabbing the money from the stash, I start a list in the kitchen, picking through the cupboards and refrigerator, pencil stuck in the corner of my mouth. The farmer's market is open today, so I pad the list with extra fruits and vegetables. As I dig through the crisper at the bottom of the fridge, I hear the apartment door shudder against the doorstop and the clumping of awkward feet on the main room floor. The list goes into my pocket.

"Hey, man, what's going on—wait, you can't—"

I step into the other room and find Vik standing over Stuart, who's kneeling in front of the open heat register. He's dusted with snow, the heat of the apartment melting it into tiny jewels in his dark hair. His boots are undone, laces soaked, tongues sticking out obscenely. The mahogany box is open on the floor.

"Nothing? There's no money?"

After recovering from a momentary paralysis at the sight of our friend, I move beside him. "What are you doing?"

"Where is it, Gail?"

He turns towards me and I actually take a step back, a hand over my mouth. He's even skinnier than when he left, with skull shadows on his face, hatless, his bare hands cracked and dry and scabbed over in a dozen places. And there's a smell, sharp, like malt vinegar gone bad.

"Jesus, Stuart," I say. "You look like—"

"The money—where is it?"

Vik and I look at each other rather than answering, which Stuart interprets as defeat. He howls and leaps to his feet with surprising agility. The shocked chemistry of withdrawal taking control of his muscles, synapses, nerves. I take a step after him; the money in my pocket feels heavy. But he hits the doorframe hard with a shallow crack rather than a solid shudder and is gone again, a few snowflakes swirling from his coat and onto the carpet as evidence of passage.

The snowstorm picks up while I'm in the market, frosting the sidewalks and lamp posts and turning the streets into a hissing, slushy mess. Early dark. A directionless wind cuts between the buildings and pushes me every which way, driving snowflakes as big as manna into my eyes and nose and mouth and gathering to melt in every fold. I'm tempted to line up at one of the chic coffeehouses and order something warm to carry with me, inhaling the vapour from the hole in its lid and absorbing warmth through its papered sides.

"No, The Collective wouldn't approve," I say to myself as I wait to cross James at Cannon, drawing a few looks from the other miserable pedestrians.

Stuart and Vik wouldn't care. Francesca would say yes to the warm liquid but not the disposable cup, as if she could enjoy them separately. I love warm paper cups, even when it's hot outside—warm liquid is more efficient at cooling a person down.

The morning I flew to Canada—I refuse to say *back* to Canada, as I never lived here before—the chai wallah's cart beckoned me for one last cup. The Delhi station was its usual seething roar of bodies, pulled clothes, outreached hands, fetid smells from toilets dumped right onto the tracks. Everyone moving and standing still, the alchemical progress of India. The vendor's kiosk was gone, survived only by the four rusted bolts that had anchored it to the platform. A surly young man had bribed his way into a new kiosk a dozen feet farther down—his chai was scorched, without character, given without comment and only after money had changed hands.

Living with Francesca has a way of making me look for warmth in my memories. As I walk north along James, I push away the warm beverage temptation and hunch deeper into my collar. Just north of the old barracks, a small crowd has gathered behind long strips of fluttering crime-scene tape. Police and ambulance lights skitter across storefronts, reflecting off snowflakes like restless, garish spirits. A trio of police officers struggles to hold a tarp against the wind, revealing glimpses of white-suited technicians working beneath floodlamps in the alley. The sidewalk is jammed, forcing me into the slurry at the edge of the road. I catch snippets of theory as I move past.

"Just a junkie—"

"No, they wouldn't call out forensics for a junkie."

"—been here since the kid found him—"

"—heard the poor little guy puked all over the side-walk—"

"Gunshot?"

"—I live above the alley, didn't hear shit—"

Sure enough, there's a boy in a filthy parka sitting on the gurney in the back of the ambulance. A female police officer sits across from him with an open notebook, looking hopeful. He's not talking, just leaning back with his eyes closed, as pale as the vehicle's artificial light. Next to him, a woman in an orange toque and puffy jacket ignores them both and studies her cellphone screen like she might find truth there.

On the far side of the crowd I step back onto the

sidewalk. Francesca is there, her back against the cobblestone wall of a restaurant, staring across James Street, unfocused. Her head is bare, glistening with a layer of snow, bringing out the redness in her face. Snowflakes land on her cheeks and melt so quickly I almost expect to see salty little puffs of steam as each one vanishes. Her uncovered hands, bluish and dry, are clasped in front of her, occasionally wringing over and around themselves without generating any warmth.

I stop in front of her, awkward, wishing for a dry spot on which to lay the flimsy fabric shopping bags. "Francesca?"

She blinks and turns towards me, her eyes slowly clearing. "Gail."

"Are you all right? Where's your hat? Your gloves?"

"I couldn't go in."

"I'm sorry?"

"The police were already here, talking to the boy. I heard him say there was blood everywhere."

She falls silent again, looking towards the crowd and the flapping blue tarp beyond, a fresh tear spilling over and disappearing into the wet beneath.

"You think it's Stuart."

"I know it is."

"Did you see him?"

"No."

Well, then, how do you know it's him? It could be anyone, I want to say. But I don't, thinking that her desire and certainty and hopefulness might combine to rule, making any logic I can apply as useless as a single wish against grief. I put the bags down and try to put my arm across her shoulders to turn her towards home. A strange moment to realize that we've never touched each other at all, even a quick hand on a shoulder or brief friendship embrace.

"Let's get moving. The walk'll warm you up," I say.

She throws my arm off and pushes me away easily. "What the hell do you care?"

"I'll make some—"

"What? Chai?"

"Sure, if—"

"Fuck your chai. I know you're leaving."

"That's not true."

"Really, Gail? A thousand dollars? First class to God knows where?"

Her words stun me and I'm unable to respond.

"Yeah, that's what I thought," she says. "Vik says he's leaving, too."

"The money, it's—"

I cut myself off. What could I say? Vik must have told her, although I can't figure why. As a distraction? Support? "Wait," I finally say. "Let's figure this out at home. I'm staying. Really."

"Bullshit."

She grabs the front of my coat and pushes me hard against the wall. The rough stones against my back, through layers of clothing, are knuckles of pain. I shouldn't be surprised at the remarkable strength her small frame can produce—an endless supply of stories about *The Purity of What Our Hands Provide* and *Working the Land*—but I am. She tightens a hand into a fist and leans it into my stomach, driving the breath from me as easily as if she has the arms of a three-hundred-pound linebacker. I drop to my knees, clutching my middle, my mouth opening and closing uselessly. She doesn't make a sound as she kneels, crushing one of the shopping bags, goes through my pockets, digs out the bundle of grocery money, and runs away.

I see a pair of black boots. A dark uniform. There's a rough voice asking me if I'm all right. I try to focus on what he's saying, which sounds like an apology for not getting to me sooner and an expression of surprise at Francesca's unexpected violence. But the oxygen is slow to return and restore the necessary balances, muddling the officer's and my words and thoughts.

"Did she steal anything? I saw her go through your pockets," he says.

"My ID's gone, so—"

My words dissolve into coughing. Misunderstanding, he reaches for the radio on his vest.

I wanted to tell him that there's no point, that I can't press charges without any ID, but he's telling me not to worry, that he got a really good look at her, that there are officers nearby who'll begin a search. Eventually, my voice will return. I'll convince them to ignore all our mischief. I'll get to my feet, lift one of the bags, and look inside. The box of Assam tea I bought from the lonely vendor at the back of the market will be ruined, the vegetables and spices crushed. All of it a mangled mess, soaking through the cheap fabric bag to drip onto my shoes and the slushy concrete. The aromas wafting upwards, surrounding me, unexpectedly full and alive against the cold, wet air.

THE ECHOES ARE ALL MINE

SAY YOU FIND a rough-looking guy living inside the marshland park where you work, and you follow your co-worker's lead when she says not to report it. Say your crush on her blinds you to the ramifications of not saying anything about the tidy campsite hidden at the far end of the rocks. Or the tall man who bolted into the woods when he saw your boat draw near.

Frankly, the decision snags like a hangnail—there's the right choice, and there's all the others, Dad used to say. Today's shift has just started and we're in the boathouse loading the gear. The skiff rests on its sling at chest level, where Mason left it last night, even though we're supposed to winch it higher.

"We need to talk about yesterday," I say.

"Why?"

"We should've called it in."

"Nah. Easier this way. Less hassle."

"But—"

"Besides, how would that look? *Uh, Sawyer, look,*" she says, her voice a falsetto, "*we slept on it last night, and today we decided to come clean—*"

"Is that supposed to be me?"

"Fuck, Isaac, we're committed," she says. "You get that, right?"

"Okay, okay. Don't get pissed."

She looks over the glittered rims of her sunglasses. "When you say *pissed*, it sounds like you're trying it on."

I look away, my ears burning. Mason has this way of getting between my seams.

"First time I've seen you wearing a dirty shirt, too," she says. "You never miss laundry night."

I resist the urge to smell my armpits and instead grab two life jackets, bailing kit, anchor. Last night I was worried about Sawyer—our supervisor—and forgot to start the washing machine. The city supplied summer staff with only three orange safety shirts, so I wash them twice a week. Mom works every night so the washer and dryer are all mine. Like the house, the TV, the echoes. I should never have told Mason about my routine. She throws the oars in so they're angled across the seats then pulls out her phone, glances at the screen.

"Break time," she says, producing a pack of cigarettes.

"It's barely eight-thirty."

"Nine o'clock somewhere."

"Sawyer said we had to get the north side done by—"

She slides a half-burnt joint from the pack. "Fuck him and his clipboard," she says.

"We could—"

"Chill out. Have a hit. We're going back first thing—"

"Wait, what?"

"—to see what we can find."

She places the joint between her lips. Her lighter is a

miniature blowtorch so her eyes, hard, glint blue against the bright jet of flame.

⤳

Say you're homeschooled but when your dad gets caught in that hydraulic press, your mom can't afford to stay home anymore. There's a move from a factory town to the city when you're sixteen. Peers who can't figure out what to say to you that isn't an insult. A summer job you like where you use a spike on a pole to pick up walking path trash, a pressure washer to deal with the goose-shit. Where the lack of interaction is a comfort. Was.

"You wanted me to pilot the boat," I say. "You should grab garbage."

Mason's stretched out along the bow bench with her head on one gunwale, legs over the other. She rolls her eyes. "Yeah, imagine heading back empty-handed."

She's nineteen. Walked away from calculus class a couple years ago and right into full-time city work. Working sanitation is a demotion, she says, but never elaborates. She likes rainbow hair dyes and hidden tattoos, and believes that a boss should never see an employee until the precise moment a shift begins. She snorts whenever she talks about the union. She told me to shut the fuck up on the first day we worked together—I don't want to know you, she said—but by the end of the month we'd traded life stories. I covered for her the day she skipped a shift and became an accomplice. Here's how I marked the milestone:

"So you owe me," I said.

"Guess so. Let me know when you want time off."

"Great. Would you like to go out—"

"No way, Home School," she said.

And Don't Ask Again, are the words I hear in my mind whenever I get distracted by her possibilities.

I throttle up the outboard and head across the marsh. Algae and lily pads crest and bob in our wake, then settle into a stillness so complete we might never have been there. Mason's eyes are closed, although she has to know where I'm going. The knurl of exposed rock and the cluster of brush nestling against the far side get larger as we draw near. I ease off and we drift along the rocks. The trees are in full summer green.

"Get the grabber," I say.

Mason stretches and fixes her eyes on the patch of wild sumac. "We're not here for the garbage."

"Right."

The current is slow, the drift easy. It seems to take an eternity to reach the edge of the brush, where it thins enough to see between the bushes. The camp looks cleaner today, a meagre pile of sundries lined up just so, the few items of clothing folded neatly. The guy has returned, reclining on a striped blanket, legs outstretched, hands behind. Skeletal. Clean-shaven. He watches us with faded grey eyes I can see from the water. The skiff's final breath of momentum carries us into shore about a dozen feet from his shoes.

"You came back," Mason says, folding her arms.

"I did indeed," the man says. "So did you."

"Wait," I whisper to the back of her head. "Are you sure you—"

"Chill, Isaac. I got this."

"You *got* this? What are you going to do?"

Mason asks how long he's been here.

"A few weeks. It's a good spot. Figured I'd take a chance on the two of you not telling anyone." He smiles. Bright, strong teeth.

"What's your name?" Mason asks. Her voice, slightly hoarse, is even and steady.

"Jacob. You?"

"Mason."

"Isaac," I say.

"Yeah, I got that. Good Bible name. Righteous."

"Why are you here?"

A harsh question, barked out. My voice. Mason turns and glares, but Jacob just chuckles and looks me in the eye. "I need the quiet."

A slight hesitation before answering, a moment to look right into me. Discover that hole, the one that's the exact shape and size of the girl at the front of the boat.

"No, that's not quite true," he says. "I like the quiet, but I need the sounds, too. The trees, the water."

"And traffic?" I ask, nodding at the highway that edges the far end of the marsh.

"White noise, probably," Mason says.

"Exactly," Jacob says.

"Not exactly peaceful," I say.

"Peace and quiet aren't the same thing," Jacob says. "A dude can find one. The other—" As his voice trails off, he pulls out a sizeable bag of weed. A blue pack of rolling paper sits among the buds, bright, a window of sky through tall trees. "Smoke?"

"No, thanks," Mason says.

"Really?" I ask her.

"How about you, Mr. Isaac?"

I shake my head.

"You're a vet," Mason says.

Jacob's eyebrows arch and he looks at her as keenly as he looked at me. "Very good, young lady," he says.

"Wait," I say. "How—"

"She saw this," he says.

He turns the back of his right hand towards me. A small parachute tattoo sits in the webbed flesh between thumb and index finger like a stain, blue-black and blurred around the edges.

"Oh. Airborne?"

Now Jacob laughs out loud, clapping his hands together. "Right on, Mr. Isaac! Solid!"

I tell him that I read a lot, speaking loudly, trying to drown out Mason calling me Home School again.

❧

"You didn't smoke with him," I say to Mason the next day. "That's not like you—"

"So you know me now, do you?"

"No, I just—No."

Eight a.m. The boathouse is already stifling. Sawyer, pissed at how little garbage we brought back, is sending us out on the marsh for an unprecedented third day.

"You figure I should get high with some nasty stranger? Get AIDS or something? No fucking way."

She goes quiet, saving me from having to call bullshit —even I can see there's more to this than hygiene. A plastic grocery bag, heavy and stretched with cans and bottles, rests on the flat floor between her feet. An uncomfortable gift. She insisted. We lower the skiff and Mason gets in the back, tilts the propeller into the murk and starts up. We don't speak on our way across the marsh.

"Shit," she says as we drift into shore. She sighs, cuts and raises the motor, steps into the shallows.

Jacob is sprawled out on his blanket. Eyes mostly closed, with just the whites visible between the slitted eyelids. Mouth wide open. The smell of vomit is sharp on the air. His shirt is up, exposing his thin belly. But the first thing you'd comment on is the spray of scars, dark keloid tissue, bursting towards his shoulders.

"He's breathing," I say.

"Passed out," she says. "OD'd, maybe."

"On what?"

"They throw bottles of pills at these guys. We should definitely call someone."

I climb ashore, leaving the anchor in the mud, and kneel next to him. The pant leg has ridden up to his knee, which is a ball of dull metal. His shin the grey weave of carbon fibre. But the angle of his foot is wrong, the leg too long. "Prosthetic," I say.

"No shit."

"It's all twisted. Has to hurt."

"It does, yeah," Mason says, her voice slower than before.

"How—"

"*Cunt.*"

"Huh?"

"It's what my dad used to call his."

We don't speak for a few moments.

"Maybe we should straighten it," I say.

"Don't—the scars'll stick."

"Scars? On the stump?"

"There are probably others, too."

"Oh. Okay."

"Gotta get the pull right. Mom had it down—me, I'd always fuck it up—" She takes a long, deep-drawn breath. "Jesus," she finally says, her voice hitching. "Ah, Jesus."

Say you wait too long to respond. You're surprised by her naked grief. Disappointed, even. So you risk becoming an accomplice again. Your phones might stay in your pockets, hers because she's too shattered, yours by choice. Would you hear yourself telling her that it's too late to say anything, that you should get back in the boat to make sure you both have a job tomorrow? Grab the bag of weed, maybe, that has fallen from the guy's pocket? Hold it out to her like it's your gift to offer?

REST

ON THE DAY Wanda Dufresne called her daughter for the last time, she woke up stiff and sore, as though her dreaming self had decided that a night of lifting small cars would be just the thing. In bed, she tensed every muscle from toe to crown, testing, the way her college swim coach had taught her, localizing the pain. Thighs, back, shoulders. Why today, she wondered. The move was weeks ago.

The strange alchemy of her internal clock, though, mirrored by the dull red digits on the clock-radio, was stable. 6:04 a.m., set just past the hour to catch the jarring babble of the morning show hosts rather than the somnolent tones of the newsreaders. The same numbers since September 4, 1982, her first day of answering phones at the Barton Jail. Wanda had retired 461 days ago and insisted that she'd never set an alarm again. Well.

The apartment was stifling; she'd forgotten to crack open the window overnight. She eased herself from her bed. Drew a threadbare flannel housecoat around her shoulders, safety-pinning it closed. Slid back the heavy curtains. The ancient, single-paned window resisted its upwards movement, its layers of old paint sticking and popping. She laid a short length of dowelling on the sill and pushed the window down to rest on it. Tom had never gotten up the nerve to confront the landlords about the excessive heat and had arrived at one inch as the perfect gap, the ideal passive-aggressive protest. "Fuck them and their old radiators," he'd said. "They can heat the outside, too."

The buzz and immediate brightness of her new mobile phone startled her. Five days ago, her daughter Melanie had begun calling at 6:06 to catch Wanda as she got out of bed. "Oh-six-oh-six," she'd said the first time. "Drop your cocks and pick up your socks, Ma. Ha ha." Dropped cocks, picked-up socks. Army-isms.

Wanda watched the call indicator on the screen, Mel's face in the background branded by her name and phone number. The ACCEPT button a big green emerald, DECLINE a ruby. There was something frightening about the urgency of these devices. Mel had bought her one, against her wishes. The ordinary corded phone in the kitchen worked just fine. Who would she call, anyhow? Tom was long gone, his ashes on the lintel, near enough if she ever had the urge to talk to the dead. Work friends already faded to nearly invisible. "Me, Ma," Mel had said. "You'll call me." Wanda had wondered aloud why her 38-year-old daughter didn't stay, then, if she was so worried about contact. But her objection had just been noise —they both knew Melanie had to find her own place.

The phone fell silent on the bedside table, its screen remaining alight for a few moments. MISSED CALL, it said.

"I know that," she said.

She took the phone from the table and slipped it into the front pocket of her housecoat, folded her arms in front of her breasts as she faced the window. It was still dark outside, December having brought its predictable, late sunrise. Through the inch of space beneath the window, Hamilton sounds let themselves in. The rush of an occasional car along Barton, early workers clutching their coffees in one hand and the steering wheel in the other, squinting at the day ahead. The muffled bark of an unleashed dog, followed by the low, resigned admonition of its owner.

"Shut up, goddammit. Some people get to sleep in."

The city was now at full speed, rushing around in its foolish, intentional way. Wanda walked downtown, a good half hour from the apartment, hoping the movement of her blood would soothe her tight muscles. She wondered whether she should make an appointment to see the doctor, although she couldn't quite imagine what he might say after she told him the soreness was from helping her daughter move out twenty-three days ago.

She sipped black, bitter coffee from a dented travel mug and frowned. Although the coffeemaker was set up every night before bed to be ready by 6:10, that morning the coffee had sat untouched for an hour before the coffeemaker shut itself off. With each sip, she told herself she should just dump the offensive brew in the gutter.

Melanie had called six more times before 7. Wanda

had ignored the alien vibrations against her thigh. Afraid to hit re-dial on the mobile, she'd used the landline to call Jim, and asked him to meet. Still half asleep, Jim had agreed, not even questioning the new location, one of those burnt-coffee chain shops everyone disliked but couldn't stay away from. She saw him enter at the far end, look around at the tile and stone interior and shake his head. He sat with a grunt, draping his filthy Carhartt coat across the adjacent table. Wanda wanted to tell him to move it—she'd wanted to say that for months, every time that coat was thrown onto her sofa on the way to the bedroom—but didn't. She talked about Mel's phone calls for a few minutes instead.

"You didn't accept any of them?"

"No. She needs to—"

"Needs to what? Get over it? Move on? She's broken, Wanda."

Wanda had a sudden and unwelcome wash of guilt. "I feel terrible about it," she said. "Now."

"I know she moved out to find herself, get some head-space, whatever, but you're her mom."

"Jesus, Jim."

"What if—if—"

"Where is this coming from? You'd come over and never say a word to her—"

"At the apartment she had you, Wanda. Now she's on her own, and you're not speaking with her."

As if on cue, the phone began to vibrate in her purse. Wanda could feel it through the table and glanced at her handbag. Jim caught her look, raised his eyebrows at her, but she shook her head. He threw up his hands in frustration. Wanda flinched.

Maybe she shouldn't have asked him to come. Mel coming to live with her had seemed so certain, so simple, in the beginning. Mel had retired from active service precisely one month before Wanda had retired from the jail and asked to move in, worried about too much time on her own. It made sense. Army support specialists, gentle officers dressed in loud camouflage, loaded her up with pamphlets and literature. Pages and pages branded either in military greys and greens or the blushing pastels of de-escalation.

"Answer the phone," Jim said.

"Look, I need my space, too. I get to enjoy my retirement."

"Fuck, answer it!"

"No. I'm sorry."

His hand flashed over the table, quick as a skink's tongue, to grab the purse. She flinched again, her neck and shoulder muscles screaming at the reflex. Jim's hands failed to find purchase, knocking the purse across the table and into Wanda's lap, out of his sightline. He swore again and stood, upsetting the table, and stormed off. Her travel mug tipped over and rolled to the edge. It hit the floor on an angle, another dent appearing on the rim. A few drops of now-cold coffee, almost black, spattered across the tile.

Wanda watched Jim's back as he pushed through the glass doors, his profile as he stalked along the sidewalk in front of the coffee shop. He disappeared at the corner. She became aware of a bearded employee standing next to the table, twisting a white bar towel like he was wringing it dry.

"Are you all right, ma'am?"

Ma'am. Mel's favourite term for her mother in sharp moments. *Yes, ma'am, if you say so!* Sarcastic. Like a teenager instead of a decorated career soldier.

"Ma'am—?"

The bearded guy was watching her closely, his towel twisting one way and then the next.

"I'm fine. It was my fault, anyway."

He looked for an instant like he wanted to argue, but instead nodded and went back behind the espresso machine, throwing an inflated Hello! at the next customer.

Wanda picked up the mug, set it back on the table, and held it in place with both hands. The cold of the stainless steel moved through her thin fingers. She looked through the window at the metal and glass building across the street, counting three stories up and four balconies from the edge. Mel had finally installed blackout curtains. Total darkness for sleeping during the day. Odd, Wanda thought, how those curtains, dark and thick, often had white liners that looked so bright from the outside.

Wanda waved her access card in front of the reader and the door released with a desultory clunk, half strength. Jake, the super, was in the lobby, halfheartedly tightening a screw in her mail slot door, blocking her passage with his bulk on the stepladder.

"Hey, Wanda."

"Will wonders never cease—"

"I know, I know."

The residents had been on him forever about the seized hinges, broken locks, doors that popped open on their own. The morning Tom died—he'd simply collapsed in front of his station at the mill without a sound, limp and dead before his body hit the concrete floor—he and Wanda had fought about the mailboxes. She'd wanted him to write to the building's owner, the city, Canada Post, anyone who could do something about the bills and letters that always ended up on the floor. He'd acquiesced. "You're right—it is criminal," he'd said. "I'll take care of it first thing."

"Sorry about this morning," Jake said.

"What do you mean—"

"Stupid dog isn't herself these days."

"Oh, that."

"This is, like, the fourth time I've had her outside today. Can't seem to decide whether to stay in or out."

"I was awake anyway."

"I think she misses Mel, actually."

"What makes you say that?"

"Never used to bark in the mornings."

Jake lived alone with his elderly Rottweiler in apartment #1 on the ground floor, and had managed to keep his duties despite the fug of weed that seeped under his door into the lobby and that he seemed to carry everywhere. Wanda imagined an uncle somewhere in the tenancy food-chain who owed a sister a favour. Mel had always liked him, much to Wanda's surprise.

"You two, always the early birds," Jake said. "You and your coffee, Mel out for her walks."

"'Marches,' she called—calls—them."

"Ha! Right! Or 'PT.' An army thing, I guess."

"Something like that."

An army of Army things, Wanda thought, all trenched up and fighting for her mind.

"Oh, wait, I forgot," Jake said, suddenly agitated. "I got something for you, just stay here."

He stepped down and disappeared into his apartment. Wanda imagined some change in her lease, some abstract new rule or guideline put in place by building owners she'd never seen. It happened often enough. Tom would shrug and roll his eyes, but he'd never complain, no matter how stupid the change was. At least, this was true outside the apartment—Wanda had received her fair share of his frustration at home. Enough to send her out the door at least twice a day, to work, a daily swim at the pool, jogging, errands. Jake emerged, forgetting to shut the door behind him, and shrugged.

"I can't find it. Sorry."

"You can just tell me, too, if—"

"No, it was from Mel. She gave it to me a ways back."

"What was it?"

"Just a letter."

"Why didn't you give it to me right away?"

Uh, I was out with Chelsea, and—"

"Chelsea?"

"My dog. You didn't know her name?"

"No."

"Oh, well, sorry. We were out early and Mel came out. Looked like she'd been crying. Gave me the envelope, said it was for you, and left."

"But why can't you—"

Jake's face went red. Studied his grubby sneakers on the faded linoleum. "I just forgot. I was pretty baked."

Growing up, Melanie wasn't a crier. Then, Afghanistan. Even after rotating home, she'd call Wanda once or twice a month, and at first the little hitch in her voice would arrive without warning, but Wanda learned to spot which types of conversations would trigger her daughter's emotions. Sometimes just a tremble in the voice, other times whole-body sobbing Wanda could feel over the phone line. Most were brief, a few seconds, but every so often Wanda would have to pull the bedcovers back hours after Tom had retired for the night. He'd wake up and give Wanda hell for using so much phone time and for pandering to their daughter's mood swings.

"Not your fault," Wanda said to Jake. "She shouldn't have put you in that position."

"I'm sure it's somewhere in there—when I find it, I'll get it to you."

"Don't go to any trouble."

Jake folded the ladder so Wanda could pass by. Chelsea, she thought. An odd name for a dog. Wanda climbed the stairs to the second floor, the pain in her thighs forcing her feet together at each step, childlike.

"Oh, and rent's due in a couple days," Jake called up. "You were late last month."

For the first time in more than thirty years, she wanted to call back. Give a girl a break. From inside her purse, her phone chirped again, as it had since she left the coffee shop. Wanda hadn't answered the calls, so now it was a barrage of text messages, each arriving to the tinny, impatient birdcall Mel had selected for her mother's text alert. Wanda pulled out her phone and counted the messages marching down the screen. Eighteen. Her thumb hovered over the REPLY bubble for a moment before she shook her head and powered off.

"Wanda—?"

"Sorry, Jake. Won't happen again."

An hour and a half later, sitting naked on a cold wooden bench in the women's change room, Wanda had her phone out again. She'd tapped out the bones of a reply, the cursor blinking *More? More? More?* after the last word she'd written. She wanted to call Melanie and tell her about the day's pain, but she only managed a text message, like the motion of her swim was still stored up in her hands, needing release, if only by manipulating a mobile phone.

The swim had helped a bit. Some healing mystery in the extension of her limbs, steadily pulling handfuls of water past her body, her heartbeat rising, warming her. The pool to herself the entire time. As she'd rested against the edge, catching her breath after fifty lengths, a lifeguard had come out to tidy up the debris on the deck leftover from the Parents-N-Tots session. Her name tag read Mason, another unusual name. She was pale and wore a fitted red YM/YWCA T-shirt over her black bathing suit, a practical but curious arrangement that produced a suggestive triangle of darkness at her crotch. Her red flip-flops looked out of character, like they should be lipstick stilettos instead. Jim would like those, she thought. Jim would notice the darkness and give it one of those terrible names men used. The girl had complimented Wanda on her technique. "Weird to see no other seniors out for afternoon lane swim, though," she'd said.

Wanda uncrossed and crossed her legs again, unconsciously shifting to keep the pins and needles away, staring at the SEND button for a long moment before opening her locker and putting the phone in her purse. She dressed slowly, savouring the space and freedom she'd had to linger without a stitch of clothing on.

She took her time walking home from the pool. She thought again about selling Tom's old car, low on its tires in the parking garage. After Tom's funeral, one of his co-workers drove it over and parked it underground for her. The keys hung on a rusty nail driven into the doorjamb, mostly unused in the fifty-one months since Tom's passing. She'd gone down a couple of times to turn the engine over and run it for a few minutes, just to keep things from seizing up, but never drove anywhere. They'd only ever needed one car—Tom drove to his job at the mill in the east end, but the jail was on Barton, a walkable five hundred metres west of the apartment for her. Maybe Jake could help her out, make sure she got a fair price—Tom would have hated her asking the super for help. An amusing thought.

She passed the jail but didn't look over at the parking lot to see who was on shift. Still couldn't ignore the orange brick they used for the exterior, bold against the decaying buildings nearby. Practically glowing. Strange choice for an urban jail, maximum security, to be so visible. Thirty-four years and eighteen days was the final tally of her time in that place, answering phones and staring first at electric typewriters then computers. Melanie practically grew up there, stopping in after school to do homework in the staff lounge, Wanda's co-workers turning a blind eye to the obvious security infraction. Called Mel *Jail-rat*, trying to be affectionate, but there was the perpetual question about how influential those uniforms and foul mouths might be. Melanie knowing by age twelve that she wanted to go military, by sixteen telling anyone who'd listen about the discipline and skill in being a combat engineer. RMC at eighteen, active duty by twenty-two. Afghanistan at twenty-eight and again at thirty, the second tour adding a detached retina, blown eardrums, flash burns from a roadside IED that killed the other two troops in the vehicle. Eight years of meds and counselling and disabled service, honourable discharge at thirty-eight. "An honourable fucking mess," she'd say. Laughing when she said it but with a dullness in the eyes. "I get asked a lot if I have bad dreams, like nightmares are the worst of it."

The soreness had returned by the time Wanda dug into the side pocket of her swimming bag for her apartment keys, creeping back into her arms and legs on the walk, a stealthy mistress letting herself back in after midnight. As she walked in, the text tone went off again, sharp against the empty hallway. Notification of a single message.

—*Never been this bad*

Wanda sat on the antique bench, sighed, and worked on a response before she could shed her winter layers. Overheated almost right away.

—You know who to call. They're there to help.

She hit SEND and remained on the bench for a long time, watching the phone, waiting for it to light up. Finally, she stood, throwing her coat onto the bench and sliding the phone into the waistband of her yoga pants. If Melanie was going to respond, she would have by now, she reasoned, as she puttered in the kitchen, wiping down spotless counters with the fetid cloth that had rested in the bottom of the sink for too long.

"She's probably calling the hotline right now," she said aloud.

Wanda moved around the kitchen, pushing bacteria around, banishing the other possibilities the instant they arose.

⸙

"I don't want to see anyone right now."

Wanda released the button and leaned against the wall next to the intercom, an old plastic unit the colour of days-old urine. Jim had arrived downstairs ten minutes before, drunk, begging to be let in.

"Come on, Wanda," he bellowed, his voice warping the speaker and dissolving into feedback.

"Jim, no. Not tonight."

"I told you I was fucking sorry."

His voice had come down a single volume level, just enough to transmit in the clear across the wires.

"No, you didn't," she said.

Wait, had he? Had she missed an apology amid the crackling and whining of the ancient circuits?

"I promise I did. Let me in, hey?"

She pushed the orange button, holding it for the requisite time, 5 seconds she hadn't had to count in more than 30 years. Then, silence, the old unit only functioning when buttons were engaged. Knowing on trust that the other party had let themselves in, the only proof the eventual knock on the apartment door.

"Let's have a drink," Jim said, brushing past her without removing his coat or his shoes.

"I don't have anything—"

"Ah, fuck, I forgot. Melanie 'too delicate' and all."

"Don't. You can't know."

In the living room, he threw his coat onto the couch and squinted at the menagerie of nail polish bottles spread across the coffee table. Wanda watched his eyes soften, tender, like the breath of his sarcasm wasn't still sour.

"You did call her. That's great—"

"I didn't."

"But—"

From across the room, next to the window, Wanda watched him process the scene. She felt a slash of cool air against her hand from the window, which she'd cracked to regulate the air in the living room with another length of purpose-cut dowelling. The bottles reflected the reading lamp, bright jewels against the mahogany table, an ascending palette of reds and maroons with a single bottle of clear base coat standing sentry amidst them. There was a glass of water, nail clippers, a trio of multi-coloured nail files, cotton swabs, a jar of nail polish remover. Wanda had worried her fingernails to the quick while waiting for Mel to call or text and decided to use the time to do them up properly, something she hadn't done in over sixteen months. Well, *do* was a bit of a misnomer when the damage was already done—camouflage the better term. Jim spent a long moment staring, likely pondering the disparity between the makeup-free Wanda he knew and the maintenance materials spread out before him. His eyes were small, uncertain.

"But you never wear that shit," he finally said.

"I don't need to, you always say."

"Why—"

More hesitation. A shake of the head. But a moment later a turn, signalled by a sly lifted chin and pursed lips.

"Well, if you didn't call her, and you're dolled up, we got the place to ourselves."

He reached down and adjusted himself through the fabric of his jeans.

"Jim, no."

"Get over here, Wanda. We'll—"

"Not tonight, I told you."

He was beside her with surprising speed, pinning her arms beside her and pushing her against the apartment door. "You smell like the pool."

He began with her neck, licking it with a rough tongue before coming up, pressing his mouth against hers. His tongue between her teeth, his stubble a thousand pinpricks on her face. Quick, heated breaths escaping like steam. He held her in place with his bulk, his left hand moving to her right breast and kneading it. When she shifted to the right to ease the weight on her lungs, Jim moaned, encouraged. The heavy pestle of his restrained erection was warm against her hip.

"The lights, Jim. Turn off the lights."

Jim reached down and unzipped himself. She didn't want to see it. Tom's You-Know-What had been a smooth and comfortable five inches, lovely in its averageness and predictable slide. Jim's was longer, thicker, bent and veined yet with a smallish purple glans that throbbed. Like a barked piece of firewood topped by a jumpy grape lollypop, she'd thought the first time he'd held her head down for a blowjob in the bright living room. "Take all of it," were his words. She'd laughed then, a sudden blend of amusement and fear, earning only a slap and a shove towards the bed, torn undies, and a rough hand over her mouth as he'd pumped and ground his hips into hers.

"Let's go from behind," he said.

He spun her around and pressed her face against the door, her cheek sticking to the old white paint, the pain in her neck flaring. He tugged at her pants, dropping them around her feet, her phone clattering along the hardwood. His calloused hands worked her underwear, scratching and catching the fabric, loud enough to hear.

"The lights," she said again.

"No."

Mel practically spit every time she said Jim's name. "He's an asshole, Mom," she said. "And dirty—is it too much trouble to shower before a date?" Wanda would shrug and tell Mel to mind her own business, that she had needs, that Tom would have hated the idea of her being lonely. It wasn't companionship but more the sex, a kind of beautiful burn. Jim's twisted architecture found every nerve spot, flinty sparks and flaring magnesium rather than the slow spread of an oil fire on water she'd enjoyed with Tom. Wanda found herself craving the scraped-out satisfaction she'd always feel afterwards. Tom was gone, work was done, and she had all this time to enjoy herself now, so why not get a little—

"Hot cock," she said out loud, surprising herself. *Cock* was a Melanie word.

Jim stopped himself as he was pulling Wanda's underwear down to her thighs.

"Huh?" he panted, his voice distant behind her.

"Drop your cocks," she said, giggling. "And pick up your socks!"

"The fuck—?"

That Melanie expression again. "Army classic," she'd call it. Wanda laughed and turned hard away from the door. She watched Jim stumble, his feet bound by his pants and jockeys, his eyes wide, the lazy right side wandering in confusion. As if he had a glass eye he'd never spoken about, which became even a funnier thing when she imagined him having to pop it in and out every morning and evening like a shooter marble in swirled glass. They could make foreplay out of it next time, hide the prosthetic around her apartment. Closet. Drawer. On the shelf next to Tom's urn. *On* the urn. Another laugh, deep and hot, overcame her and she had to put a hand against the wall. A rushing in her ears. Jim called her something familiar and terrible, but this time the word was as blurry as his denied hand rushing up towards her face. Closed, this time.

Tender swelling against her temple and ear, but no pain anywhere else. Shoulders and neck fine. Like the soreness had been knocked clear. It was now dark in the apartment, the only light slitting in through the apartment door, left open whenever Jim had left. A cold draft slid along the floor and around her bare legs. She got up and stretched, marvelling at the limberness in her neck and shoulders, and closed the door against the chill.

The closing door revealed a white envelope that had lain hidden from her view between door and hallway. Her name scrawled in blue ink across the front, barely legible. Jake's hand, for sure—Mel's handwriting was as precise as her sense of time. Wanda bent to pick it up, lingering at the lowest point of her movement. No pain there, either.

She should feel like she'd just given birth to a back-labour child, the strain bursting the blood vessels in her eyes and swelling every muscle in her shoulders, neck, and face. After breaking Wanda's waters near the start of a city-stopping blizzard, Melanie had taken thirty-six hours to greet the world and left her mother incapable of holding out a hand even for Tylenol. "That swim strength came right back when you needed it," Tom had said as the doctors and nurses snipped and weighed and ministered to the newborn, an unnamed bundle of vernix and misshapen proportions. He'd barged into the delivery ward and insisted on remaining in the room in a rare display of outward stubbornness. The blizzard-stretched medical team had shrugged, too exhausted to call security. Wanda and Tom waited seven days to name their baby girl, by then her limbs stretched to their trembling length, her head its proper shape.

She turned back towards the empty apartment.

"Well, what to do with myself today, eh?"

The apartment didn't reply. In the living room, the nail polish bottles were undisturbed on the coffee table. She'd left one bottle open, forgotten when Jim arrived, its brush laid on the table nearby. The delicate glitter of Starruby Red fully cured and hard in the bristles. Mel's favourite colour. Oh, shit, she thought. She went back to the hallway and searched for the phone, finally locating it beneath the old bench. The metal corner had been dented, but the screen powered right up. A single notification, time stamped from hours before. A single text.

—*Please*

Wanda stared at the word, its lack of punctuation an IED crater beside a rutted road. She tucked the envelope under her arm and grasped the phone with both hands, her fingers stuttering across the screen's awkward patterns of unlocking, locating, opening. The phone warmed as it processed. She jabbed at the emerald CALL button four times before it responded, disappearing against Mel's smiling contact photo when she answered. The call-duration digits ascending from 00:00:00, a kind of rest state, one digital second at a time.

BUDDY'S MIRROR

YOU WAKE UP *and feel like you'll never be able to tell the difference between the grey clouds and the smoke. Your head aches so bad you dream about puking. The stench is so thick you swear you could roll it between your fingers like Plasticine. You're sweating hard and you worry about heat stroke as you pee yellow, so yellow, like syrup. Tiny needles of itching threaten to rip your crotch to bits. Your socks are more thread than fabric, and no matter what you try you can't wash the salt stains from your armpits.*

You think about dying.

Not enough to kill yourself, but enough to know that sometimes suicide's not as crazy as everyone thinks it is. You know for a fact you're not crazy. The chaplain says that everyone deals with mortality in different ways. Everyone. As though you weren't alone. As though Buddy sitting next to you is scratching himself and thinking the same thing.

And that's what gets your ass out of the sack every morning, ready to face the same windowless walls that ache to kill you.

I didn't believe Buddy when he told me. Sat me down and laid it all out, like a guru who'd seen it all. As though I'd climbed the highest peak to see him rather than just up the elevator and past the nursing station. Amazing how young he was. I don't want to sound cliché but, man, they were right when they said you could read it in their eyes—you couldn't stuff anything more mechanical into his skull. When he talked it was as though his emotions had been replaced with cement. He just talked and stared and scratched. The antibiotics had killed the infection. The memories still made him claw at himself.

"My decision was purely financial," I said. It was hard to shock mom and dad. "But what about school," they'd asked. I told them that the registrar had intervened and promised to re-register me when I returned: "Good for you. They need you over there," the grey man behind the desk had said and then returned to his paperwork.

Dad was more careful. "I know you volunteered," he said. "You don't have to go." I told him it was a part of being a soldier. I told him that they needed medics and that I wanted to go. I told him that it wasn't combat it was peacekeeping. I told him I wouldn't be part of it. I told him about the money: basic rate plus isolation pay plus danger pay plus displacement allowance, and it was tax free. My dad hated taxes, as though the danger and isolation were secondary. So that's the argument I adopted. "It's good money," I'd say to anyone who asked, "and it looks good on my resume."

But my professional prospects were as far from my decision as the registrar was. I had never forgotten granddad's face the day he died: grey, dry, lined. For the first time since adolescence he'd had a shave in the afternoon, and folded hands, the irony of the peaceable atheist. The way his skin was cool to touch, not cold like people said, cool. Before, I had always enjoyed those wrinkling valleys and the sandpaper stubble of his face when he spoke; its new stillness was as unfamiliar to me as the surface of the moon. I pulled a chair up and sat with him for an hour.

I wanted to see what real death was like. The way it *really* is, not like CNN's jumpy images of grainy explosions and after-the-fact cleanups: so distant, so sanitized, so clean. I would love to explain it, but no one asks. People wouldn't have understood my real reasons, like there's no way to see it without participating in it.

But it's impossible not to be a part of it, really. Six months of training then off you go. Great promises of worthiness, as though the world should stand and applaud our nobility on the six o'clock news.

We'd arrived in late afternoon. The bunker was new. No ventilation yet. Hot. It smelled of canvas and rubber as we trundled in with cots, foot powder, sleeping bags, barracks-boxes, rifles, pillows, rucksacks, radios, ammunition, web-gear, soap, toothpaste, gas-masks, flip-flops, pictures, and det-cord. We had new desert boots, new helmets, new blue berets, new satellite-phones, new pistols, new underwear, new all-weather matches, and new field caps. I had new combats, new body-armour, new socks, a new blue ball cap, new rain gear, new pens, new medical bag, and new red cross stickers to put on everything. They promised to send stencils and spray-paint for the final, permanent red crosses. I put one on my first letter home, reassuring, as though it was bulletproof.

"Get squared away," McNicoll had said, like he'd been there longer than we had. We just sat there and sweated, draped over our piles of gear like khaki tarpaulins.

"It's Eastern Europe, for God's sake, why's it so hot?" Buddy in the far corner asked. I felt dizzy and sick from unloading the truck; my first casualty, I thought, and I hadn't even unpacked my sleeping bag. I drained my canteen, slung my rifle, and went out to grab an extra water jerry.

It took me almost an hour. The bunker was cooler when I got back. Some engineer had rigged a meat-locker fan between the sandbags and the roof. Sacrifice: one window. Somehow everyone had sacked out despite the constant whining from the overtaxed fan-motor. Loud as hell, but it cooled us off. I unpacked my gear alone.

That night, McNicoll said that the CO hadn't known we'd arrived. Strange baptism, it seemed, to be forgotten. So we went to bed early; cool enough to sleep, a bunch of snoring cocoons lying in the dusty corners of a bunker a million miles from anyone we knew. The fan noise drowned out the snoring. I dreamt of red crosses and high school and meat locker fans whining, whining, whining.

I lay awake as the bunker grew stuffy and smelled of sleeping men. Buddy ran through the door yelling, "Stand to! Stand to!" He was very concerned. His flashlight flitted from face to face, and he fidgeted while we dressed in the dancing flashlit darkness, groggy and bleary. Pants. Shirt. Boots. Helmet. Pistol. Buddy looked at Buddy then Buddy for instructions. Confusion. No one moved. McNicoll, in charge, swore, grabbed his web-gear and stormed out, half dragging the offending soldier, leaving me in charge. The fan whined on. I turned on my flashlight; its red filter dimly illuminated a half-dozen expectant faces looking for guidance. I heard myself tell them to hold tight, then walked out.

We hadn't heard the shot that killed Buddy. One of the local civilians we hired to work for us. A cook, maybe. Caught him on the way back from the latrine, buttoning up his jeans. McNicoll and an anonymous lieutenant shone their flashlights on Buddy all sprawled in the dirt as cold as a museum exhibit. Some French medic administered CPR. He stopped, shook his head and sat back. The bullet had caught Buddy under the brim of his ball cap, which lay in the dirt a few feet away. No one returned the sniper's fire. The rules said that we weren't allowed to unless he shot at someone who wasn't already dead. We stood around waiting for the sniper to decapitate someone else. He didn't. Buddy just lay there, obscenely splashed with white light as his brains soaked into the ground.

I stayed and watched while Buddy was zippered into a body bag then went back to bed, my introduction to violent death fading like a bad movie.

You can't imagine the anticlimax. Months of anticipation, intense training, and all you do is walk the same patrol route day in, day out, hoping that someone doesn't feel like blue-helmet target practice. Sometimes, you get to ride the white iron horses bristling with virgin weapons. They shoot over *you at each other. You crawl over the landscape, fat, white maggots peaceably cradling your rifles and hoping never to use them or even imagine the reality of where you are.*

I'm looking at my third case of heat exhaustion. Buddy complains about the treated water: "Hate that shit. Smells like a fucking swimming pool," he says. I forgo yet another medic's *I-know-best-so-listen-to-me* speech and give him my best *don't-fuck-with-the-heat* look.

"I forgot to drink," he says. "Landmines, you know."

A cow had triggered a bounding-mine the day before, cutting its owner clean in half. The old man had lain beside the crossing, dead and bloody, while nearby his cow stood against a fence, its side torn open by shrapnel, trying to graze but too weak to do so. The old farmer had been a lost cause so I did what I could for the cow. Sacrifice: two 9mm rounds between the eyes and a chunk of my psyche for watching a cow live through the first bullet. The quartermaster had looked surprised when I handed him my magazine short two rounds, then laughed when I told him. I hadn't thought it was funny.

"I know," I tell Buddy, who's not interested in my memories and whines about the water and his growing dizziness.

The road's melted, and our section walks on the shoulder. The guys are edgy. Gravel's the best for hiding landmines, so the engineers sweep the shoulder first. Slow. Irony spills into our labours: this is what we call "quick-time country," open and dangerous.

➳

Every now and again a forgotten landmine vaporizes some unlucky soul, and your patrol stops. The reporters stand off a ways as though they're at a barbeque, away from the smell of charred flesh and shit. You act as though you could ever get used to that smell, and give your candy to dirty, bloodied children and hope it helps.

So death grabs you slowly, gradually. You feel it pulling gently, the way you crave cigarettes. An extra look here, a longer pause there. You don't even realize it.

➳

I'm thinking about how thankful I am that I'm not infantry: months of patrols, stopping, starting, waiting for your tax-free million-dollar round. Long hours spent pacing between two armies who don't care if you're in the way. Almost never shooting back, never really knowing the satisfaction of real combat.

I am glad that I'm as restricted as I am; I'm almost not allowed to think about combat. So I fix people. Medical thinking helps pass the time: save some, lose others.

I move the salt tablets to the top of the bag and wonder if I'll lose anyone from heat stroke. No matter how many times I lecture them, they're always forgetting to drink enough water. "Heat stroke'll kill you just as dead as bullets," I say. They nod and smile and forget about it two days later. Buddy from Bravo had cried just before he went into a coma—his body had shut down hours before we sent him to the field hospital. There's nothing harder to watch than a man cry without tears. He made it back to Canada. Probably.

McNicoll calls a halt and stands in front of me, sweating. I notice the large salt-stains on his body-armour and pull out a salt-tablet.

"I can't believe this heat," he says, swallowing the tablet dry. "How many guys are down?"

I tell him.

He grunts then looks at the overcast. "It's not supposed to be this hot. Indian summer, we'd call it. Wonder what it's called here?"

I say I don't know. A white helicopter chatters by towards the buildings on the horizon. McNicoll seems to be waiting for something as we shift uncomfortably. I imagine we must look strange, a small army of green with bright blue helmets waiting beneath the umbrella of someone else's war. I notice for the first time that I can't hear gunfire.

"It's quiet today," I tell McNicoll.

I almost expect him to say that it's too quiet, like in the movies. It feels like a movie, what we're doing, moving frame by frame and hoping the film stays on its guides. McNicoll says nothing. He's edgy too, unhappy about the necessity of waiting in the open. I keep moving, restless, to stave off boredom. Salt tablet here, foot powder further down the line for jock itch, ibuprofen for the strained knee that I think is bad enough to send Buddy home. We wait for the engineers to finish their sweep and pray that the screen writers don't pencil in a mortar round.

The artillery rounds screaming overhead sound like freight-trains. We never hear the guns in the valleys, just the wailing, an eerie reminder of our fragile steps under this deadly sky. Buddy looks up at the sound and shudders; unease, contagious, ripples through the section.

"Like waiting for the sky to fall and not wearing a fucking raincoat," someone yells.

McNicoll gives Buddy in front a shove. "Move."

The buildings grow. Our spirits fade. We weave through twisted concrete, craters, and pockmarks, the staples of village life. Hunched figures move through the wreckage, spirits that drift through the constant haze. These are the few brave souls. Others seek privacy in the corners and holes, away from our unfamiliar eyes and safe from random bullets. We feel the same way. A bond. A growing mental reprieve from the destruction and the graffiti. Growing. Like cancer.

The section tenses as we pass the first ruins. Speed is a new enemy; it blinds a person here, where nooks and holes are both refuge and danger. "Never look where your weapon's not pointed," I remember from Basic. I finger my holstered pistol and stroke the red cross on my bag.

The echoed shooting reaches every ear simultaneously. Sounds bounce off the walls and shattered buildings, piercing and surrounding us, as though we've been thrown blindfolded into a concert hall. McNicoll fondles his rifle, clicking his safety on and off. Once. Twice.

You know they're not shooting at you. Doesn't matter. You get to cover and try to be invisible. You almost wish they would so you could do something. It's like porn—you only watch.

We're bathed in gunfire that drives noise into our bellies —it's not like the movies at all, polite machine-gun chattering in your ears. No, you feel it in your gut the way you feel boxing gloves. Gunpowder stings our nostrils as we feel bullets smack into the walls inches from where we've pressed ourselves. I'm caught between studying the pattern of pockmarks in the wall and trying to melt into it when McNicoll collapses next to me.

"Jesus," he yells.

"What the hell's happening?" I shout in his ear. I wonder if he can hear my voice crack.

"Somebody's making a push," he says. Red tracers streak like lasers between the buildings and over our heads. So fucking close. Never been this close before—are they shooting at us? One in five's a tracer; I'd never see the other four. The antenna from Buddy's radio dances as McNicoll yells at the crackling voice in the handset. He yells something in my ear about spacing. I can barely hear him. My head feels as if it'll split my helmet and I'm caught between screaming and puking. My eardrums must be bleeding—I hope McNicoll can hear me.

He shakes his head. "We gotta wait it out."

"But they're shooting at us," Buddy with the radio yells. McNicoll doesn't answer. I know what he'd say, though: we'd be in a lot more trouble if they were.

McNicoll points at Buddy behind the concrete flowerpot and shouts. Buddy starts as though his parents had just caught him with his hand up some girl's shirt. I see where McNicoll wants him ("Damn flowerpot wouldn't stop a snowball," he adds). Buddy gets up and runs across the street, hands over his crotch like he's facing a penalty-kick. The shot stops him. I watch his hands—they're still stuck in his groin—as he folds face-first into the pavement. Someone broke the rules, I tell myself, as Buddy lies in the middle of the street like a pothole.

McNicoll drags Buddy under cover; I hear a snap as a bullet catches him in the shoulder. He's a stone, not a noise even though the pain must be unimaginable. So silently he drips blood all over Buddy. Buddy doesn't care. I see the others looking. They know Buddy getting tagged makes them statistically safe, but they'd gladly crawl through McNicoll's exit wound to get away. I'm mentally writing out forms in triplicate as McNicoll slumps, faint, against our wall. Somehow he finds voice enough to yell about conserving ammunition. I try not to tell him about the fist I could stick through the hole in his shoulder.

Buddy down the line points and yells, jumps up— McNicoll wants to scream at him but can't—and empties his magazine into a dark, crumbling window. We're not here for this, I know. We're here to watch, not shoot at blind buildings. I should say something. I'm second in command but there's no way they'd listen to me now. I catch blurred movement out of the corner of my eye as the section storms the building. Fuck.

I hope the shooter is dead before they get there. Building assaults. Bloody and fatal. I hate them more than syphilis.

My hands are gloved, yet I can still feel the warmth of McNicoll's blood as I rip open a field dressing. I'm alone with McNicoll and Buddy whose eyes are wide open as though he expects me to say something. I know that it's not quiet, but I can't hear the violence—I've sucked myself into a soundproof tube. My headache seems out of place, a holdout, hung over. I feel as if I've had my ears boxed; my field of vision jumps and dances as though I'm watching through a handycam. Through the ringing, I sense an explosion of light and noise as I tighten McNicoll's field dressing. I have to do this right, I say to myself, I'll be damned if I lose McNicoll from a shoulder-wound. A puff of air, a first-kiss breath, brushes against my cheek as I stuff McNicoll's shoulder with dressings. God, that stings, I think as I see drops of blood—my blood?—on McNicoll's sleeve. McNicoll points suddenly behind me—he's trying to bring his rifle around but can't because of his wound.

I don't even think. My virgin pistol is suddenly in my hand and roaring, pounding, kicking. I'm willing the bullets through the barrel at somebody—anybody—and I'm yelling as if I'd been insulted in a bar fight. I point and point and point and pull until I'm clicking at nothing but empty street. I turn back to McNicoll and add another bandage, swearing to myself that I'm not ready for this shit.

McNicoll places his good hand on my wrist and stares at something behind me. I look, and for a moment think that Buddy has moved. But the eyes are closed. There are no lines on the grey, peaceful face. His camouflaged green hat is askew, and covers his long, dark hair and the smear of blood on his jaw. His AK-47 leans against him and its bayonet digs into the asphalt. It's not Buddy, but he's dead all right, his uniform mottled with wet, black spots. McNicoll looks at the pistol in my hand and at the body.

He's trying to speak, I know, but I'm distracted by my pistol's unfamiliar warmth. I'm saying things to him now, about being okay and help is on the way and I'm looking at his dog tags and looking for the radio operator I'm looking everywhere at once but I can't look further down the street at the man I've killed.

I wonder about what I've done and I don't really feel anything other than the blistering adrenaline in my veins. I'm amazed at my indifference and lack of philosophical reflection. Calmly, yet with my hands distantly shaking, I pop out the magazine, notice that it's empty, drop it, rustle through my web-gear, and slide in a new one. The reporters are still cowering behind us, retreating into their scratch-pads and clicking cameras. I turn back to McNicoll's wound, noting absently that I'll have to answer for what I've done. Maybe a medal, maybe something more serious.

But above all, I count the missing rounds in my head and I wonder what I'll say to the quartermaster because God knows I can't stand to have him laugh at me again.

❧

You feel like you should be excited, or jittery, or ashamed. You get home a few months later and people saw it on the news and everyone wants to know what it's like. Only you can't tell them, because you weren't really there. It was some-one else that drew his weapon without thinking and took a life. It was someone else who, after, struggled to keep McNicoll alive long enough to get to the hospital, forgetting about the violence of death and the smell of blood on his uniform. You can't explain this, because there's no way to make it sound real, no way to explain how survival is a kind of escape. And yet they want it all, as though you can eject the video and run it for them in their family-room. Rewind. And again.

The right thing, the wrong thing. Doesn't matter now, even though months and years have filled the gap, and reflection is only as clear as the day itself, blurry and blotchy. There's no line, no boundary. And all you keep thinking as you stare and fade away that the only difference between then and now is that by now the pistol barrel's cooled down and you could put it back into your holster if you wanted to.

WITH SUCH A THING

DARBY FROWNED. THE paint was not responding well to the cold. He laid the small fan brush across the palette, blew warmth onto his hands, and laid back across the scaffolding's workworn planks. He pulled out his phone, the screen's bluish glow bright in his eyes, and thumbed Redial. One ring. Two. Three. Click.

"Darby."

"Arthur."

"It's late."

"I could use a heater. Paint is slowing up."

A grunt. "You're supposed to supply everything yourself."

"I know, but—"

An involuntary pause, just before the excuses. His tiny walkup on Barton way out in the east end. Bus fare. Old, old bones. And so on. Darby heard Arthur moving on the line, a rustle audible over the hiss of traffic bleeding through stained glass, foil came, tarnished solder. He imagined his friend levering his bulk forward in the musty recliner Darby himself had fallen asleep in a few times, the persistent smell of cigars and books, mahogany shelves and candlelight. What a retired priest filled his winter evenings with. Knowledge and fine things.

"Ah, forget it," Darby said. "I'll figure it out. Sorry to disturb you."

"Keep your pants on. Gimme twenty minutes. I have an old heater somewhere—"

Darby wanted to argue but didn't. The deadline was too close. And corporations love to block payment when a deadline is missed, especially if it's an old guy working for nothing rates who can't afford a countersuit. Arthur had told him not to worry about it, that he'd look out for him, but Darby still worried.

"All right," he said. "Thanks."

He flipped the phone closed. There was the faintest paint smell in the air, the cold reducing everything the senses could take in. Restoring the demons and gargoyles was taking the longest, their unorthodox golds and browns as at odds with each other as they were with the cherubs and other heavenly icons spanning the vaulted ceiling. Old work. The date on the signature in the far corner was more than a hundred and twenty years ago, although that would have been the completion date. Maybe a decade of effort prior, if the artist's other works were any measure. Why he tucked these grotesques—two gargoyles, two demons—at the highest point is a mystery, their fiercely posed, twisted expressions hidden by century-old soot until Darby uncovered them a year ago. The highest spots usually reserved for the holy.

By the time Darby climbed down to the sanctuary floor, further numbing his hands on the scaffolding's steel piping, Arthur had arrived, and had seated himself next to the kettle of water Darby kept on the old milk crate in the corner. When he saw Darby, he made to rise from the stool but Darby waved him back down.

"Gotta keep moving, anyhow," Darby said.

"Blood and paint slowing right down, eh?"

"Yeah."

"Tea?"

"You need to ask?"

Arthur threw a tea bag into each of the two chipped mugs.

"Why don't you bring in another stool so we can have a proper sit-down?"

"Too much like work," Darby said. "Besides, I spend all day on my ass."

They watched the kettle boil, and didn't speak further as the water was poured and the tea steeped, and through the first few sips, shallow, to avoid the scald.

"Brought an extension cord, too," Arthur said.

"Already have one."

"The heater'll need its own. Blow a fuse, otherwise."

"Right. Thanks."

"How much longer do you figure?"

"Deadline's in just over a week. But—"

"The part you left for last is a bugger, yeah, I know."

"Soot takes a long time."

They looked over the brims of their mugs at the interior of the church, cleared out for the restoration, the oak pews being refinished somewhere else. The place hadn't seen a congregation in years but its heritage designation had bullied promises out of its new owners, a condo corporation developing every other square inch of the property and meting out restoration funds in painfully small amounts. Arthur's status as the parish's last vicar had allowed him to recommend Darby for the work, but not get him any more money to do the job, even when it became clear it was a tough one.

"Got a favour to ask," Arthur said after a while. "Grandson of an old army buddy needs some work."

"Why're you asking me?"

"Kid got his discharge."

"So?"

"Was in Afghanistan. Kandahar."

"Ah, Jesus. Tough go."

"No parents, just a grandpa, an old geezer who still likes his war stories."

"Like us."

"Yeah, like us."

Darby laughed and shook his head. "Buddy getting another favour from the chaplain," he said.

"They go both ways."

"I have a feeling everyone mostly owes you."

Arthur made a dismissive motion with his free hand. Familiar, without thinking. Arthur was the only person Darby ever knew who bore humility as it was supposed to be borne—from the bones outward, good marrow feeding the blood, sinews, skin.

"Is there anyone you didn't serve with? Some retirement."

"That's rich, coming from you," Arthur said.

"I was painting long before I signed on that line—"

"Sure, sure. '... And I'll do it 'till I die.' You need new material."

"We both do."

"Maybe. Wouldn't know where to look, myself."

They met on a rainy day in Korea in 1953. Both late for mass. Arthur was freshly posted to the tiny airfield, jet-lagged and stunned by the mud and squalor. Darby, hungover and looking for a place to vomit, turned a corner too quickly and ran right into the padre. Ended up guiding him to the chapel tent and sitting through mass. After, they shared a small bottle of Darby's black-market soju and made it a weekly thing until they rotated home at the end of the war. Stayed in touch, though Darby got out as quick as he could and Arthur kept his uniform on for a long time. Eventually they ended up in the same city, Arthur retiring from the army chaplaincy to civilian priesthood, shepherd to a dwindling parish of grey hair while Darby painted houses, furniture, whatever to stay afloat.

"So he paints, then," Darby said. "Useless to me if he doesn't."

"Bit of a prodigy, apparently."

"I can't pay him. My margin's pretty thin—if I get paid at all."

"You will. I said I'll take care of it. This, too."

"You say so."

"I do."

"All right then."

The men sipped a while in silence. Darby shuffled his feet, set his mug onto the crate.

"Thanks for the heater."

"It was just sitting in the basement. Besides, you'd freeze up, make me look bad—"

Arthur's final words dissolved into a flurry of coughs. Deep. The kind a guy can't fight, that bend him over and turn him inside out, the kind he'd rattle wetly into a handkerchief and hide before anyone can see. A dark handkerchief, one of many. Bought just for.

"Always complaining," Darby said, avoiding eye contact as his old friend composed himself.

"Get back to work."

"I should, yeah."

"I'll bring the kid by tomorrow."

"What's his name?"

Arthur simply waved a farewell, leaving Darby to face another few hours of fine line work high above and wondering what kind of man the boy would turn out to be.

After work the next day, after the heater and cords and paints had been stored in the altar cabinets, Darby took the kid out for a beer. They walked slow along John Street, Darby comfortable carrying his limp and the kid shuffling behind with his hands shoved deep into the pockets of his camouflage parka. Arthur—who still drove the parish's car, which had been retired too—had brought him by late in the day while Darby was up in the scaffolding, so he hadn't had a chance to measure the boy properly. James, his name was. Not Jim or Jimmy or Jamie. James. Five-foot-eight at most and average in build and stature. Deepset eyes, dark and hard. Barely said a word.

"You could've done a little work today," Darby said, to make conversation.

"I'd like to watch for a while." An average voice, too, if a bit on the quiet side.

"Look, I'm not sure how much Arthur's told you, but the toughest work is done."

"Hate to rush in."

"You'll be fine."

"You set the tone, sir. I'll follow."

Darby felt the old enlisted man urge to snap at the kid, *Don't call me sir! I work for a living!* but kept his tongue. Having served, James would've heard the joke a million times, but he might not find the humour in it now. Difficult when you're fresh back to the world and everything looks different.

"Tomorrow, then," Darby said.

"Sure, tomorrow."

The bartender nodded at Darby when they came in. He was an old vet himself, sowbellied and balding, greasy apron and a notable set of bluing tattoos on his forearms. A few steps and he was behind the taps, drawing a pint into a cloudy Labatt's glass, the navy blue letters fringed in faded gold. He simply grunted at Darby's two raised fingers and had the beer in front of them by the time their coats were off and they'd settled on the stools.

"Who's the kid?"

"He's doing some work with me over at the church. James, Saul. Saul, James."

"Hope Blue's all right," Saul said to James. "Darby won't touch anything else."

"It's fine," James said. "Wet and cold. All you need."

"I like him already," Saul said, and moved down the bar to fill another order.

James raised the glass, looked into the suds, and drained half the pint with a single long draught. Darby raised an eyebrow.

James caught the look. "Beer's for drinking, right?"

"True enough."

"Still, ever try anything else?"

"There a problem with Blue?"

"It's all right. Not the strongest, though."

"Don't understand why beer needs to be strong."

James gave a small smile. "Figured a military guy would get it."

"Military's why I don't drink more than Blue."

"I don't—"

"Too much trouble in it."

They fell silent for a few minutes and drank. Darby watched James drain his beer with his next effort, Saul appearing just as the glass was set back on its cardboard coaster, offering another. James nodded.

"How do you know Major Fildes?"

Darby chuckled. "'Major Fildes.' Haven't heard that in a while."

"That's what grandpa called him. A long time, then."

"Since Korea. Posted to the same airfield. He was base chaplain, I tinkered with the planes."

"Oh."

"Oh, what?"

"The Major said that you'd seen some shit, so I—"

"You assumed I was Army."

"Right."

"I was an airman. Machinist. We were strafed a few times from the air, shelled once from offshore. Lost some guys," Darby said, hesitating slightly at the memory. "Not *in* the shit, but still ugly."

"Ugly's a good word for it."

"Yeah."

"At least the war left you with a trade—"

"Should've. Couldn't look at the machines after-wards."

Another pause. Longer, this time.

"Uh, so now you paint," James said.

"I always did, but as a hobby before the war. Keeps me quiet, mostly." Darby raised his glass. "To leaving it behind," he said.

"Fuck, yeah."

They dipped the rims of their glasses towards each other and drank. A Drunk's Curtsey, the boys used to call it. Quicker for getting stuck in—no messing around with the clink-clink-clink of useless courtesy. James downed his second as quickly as he had the first. Darby took a single sip and set his glass down. An old habit, nursing his beer. After Korea, he ran around for drink a bit too much, saw some trouble until he met his wife—now long dead of the cancer that kills a woman nearest her heart—and suddenly had a reason to limit himself. Still did. James ordered another, observed his own set ritual of the briefest of pauses, a hard stare at the foam and beer, before a long drink, a deep consumption. Over the next hour, he put five down before Darby'd finished his one. Darby looked at his watch.

"It's late," Darby said. "See you tomorrow?"

"You will."

"All right to get home?"

"Never had trouble before."

Darby stood, knotting his scarf under his chin and shrugging on his coat. There was an awkward moment where he waited for James to get up before it became clear that he wasn't going anywhere. Darby said good night and walked to the end of the bar, paid Saul for all six beers, asked him to keep an eye on the boy. The bartender rang the bills into the register, mumbling something about not being the police, that he wasn't in business to babysit his customers. When Darby hesitated for a moment, Saul waved him away and growled at him not to worry, that he'd take care of it.

The next day, Arthur brought the kid in two hours late without an explanation. The priest had to stop halfway across the stone floor to cough, racking himself double and hawking something nasty into his handkerchief. Eyes red and watery by the time he stood below the scaffolding, making Darby want to go down, put his arm around Arthur, and help him onto that solitary stool. James following a few paces behind, eyes clear, unaffected by the previous night's drinking. He didn't apologize for his lateness.

"You're sounding worse and worse," Darby called down.

"Nothing rest and a leisurely bath can't cure," Arthur said.

"Can't see you getting much of either."

"A cup of your finest brew, then."

"Kettle's broke. The cold, I think."

"Ah. Too bad."

Darby had opened the church as the sun was getting high enough to kiss the stained glass at the top of the church's gothic arches. Waited next to the cracked plastic kettle for long enough to feel the chill before realizing the little light had never come on.

"Should leave the heater on tonight," Darby said.

"Developer'd have a cow about the hydro."

"They'll never know. Haven't seen anyone from corporate in months."

"Thank God for that—they seem to call me every other day."

"About me?"

A pause. "Yeah."

"And—?"

"Don't worry about it. Above your pay grade."

"Ha, ha."

"You have enough for the kid to do?"

"I asked you not to call me that," James said.

"Oh, he speaks!" The remark accompanied by a mock expression of surprise.

"I hate it when—"

"Cry me a river, troop. And call me 'Sir.'"

James glared at the priest for a long moment before giving a low chuckle. "Sure, sir. Yes, sir. Thank you, sir."

Arthur sniffed and ambled out without another word.

"That was out of line," Darby said.

"Officers have thick skin, everyone knows that."

"You might just say thanks next time."

James, hands deep in his parka's pockets, looked

around the sanctuary. "Can't get over how much bigger it is in the daylight," he said.

"Did you hear me?"

"Sure."

Darby swallowed what he was going to say next. Something unhelpful and biting. "You coming up? I could use a hand."

"Give me a minute."

But when James claimed to the top of the scaffolding, his hands were empty. He refused to go back down for the supplies Darby had set out for him, saying he was content to watch a while longer. Darby still said nothing. Best to let him set the tone. If Darby tried too hard, James would tuck himself deeper into his parka and throw up a wall of quiet anger. At ten o'clock Darby sent James out for some tea from the cafe around the corner, but he came back an hour later with two cups of Tim Hortons' coffee, the nearest of which was at least a click away. Black. Cream and sugar in a bag on the side. Darby could smell the cheap, foul brew before he got down to the floor.

"I ordered tea."

"It's still warm—made them double the cups."

"Not much of a coffee drinker."

"Leave it, then. I'll drink it later."

"No, it's fine. I'll just drown it in cream and sugar."

James drew a couple of creamers out of the bag and tossed them over. He pocketed all the sugar packets except one, which he tore open and poured right into his mouth before dropping the empty sachet to the floor. As Darby was about to say something about it, James lifted a coffee from the paper tray, opened the lid, and walked over to the far side of the sanctuary, stepping hard on the empty sugar packet. Darby could see the coffee's steam rising above James's shoulder as he moved. He stopped at the far wall, reached up to where the artist's signature rested above a cornice, and ran his finger across the faintly textured script.

"Why do you think he put the monsters so high?"

"Sorry?"

"The gargoyles."

"Must've had his reasons."

"You never wondered?"

Of course I did, Darby thought, still annoyed at the jagged miscues James had begun tossing in a pile between them. What artist wouldn't?

"The colours are all wrong, too," James said.

"You think I should've changed them?"

"On the way here Major Fildes talked about your gift."

"Gift."

"How you can make any painting look like new."

"He's no art critic."

"He said the same thing, actually."

James took a sip, the sound echoic in the motionless air, and returned to where Darby had taken a seat on the solitary stool. His face had eased somewhat, the pinched skin between his eyes relaxing as he continued to scan the mosaics and stonework. Enjoying himself, Darby realized.

"Arthur told me about the scholarships," Darby said.

"A few, yeah. Not enough, though."

"Army's good for that. The money, I mean."

"Money wasn't enough, either."

"Art school must be pretty expensive."

"Huh?"

"Arthur said you were an artist."

"I don't—"

James stopped himself, shook his head and gave a low, quick laugh, as bitter as the cooling coffee in Darby's hand.

"Art school, of all things," James said. "Why the fuck would he say that?"

"I don't understand."

"He knew it was a rugby scholarship."

"So no—"

"Fly-half. Outside. I was fast."

"Oh."

"I couldn't draw a stick figure to play hangman with, to be honest."

James laughed again, lower this time. Darby heard wonder in it.

"He told you it was art school. And you bought it. God, that's—that's—"

James didn't finish. He simply moved away, drew another sugar packet from his pocket, crumpled its contents into his mouth, and tossed it to the floor. From across the sanctuary, Darby could hear the grinding of individual grains against the kid's teeth as he chewed.

꒳

James showed up on his own the next day. On time. He helped Darby set out the cans of paint, Varsol, brushes. He ran the heater and the cord up to the scaffolding by himself, turned on the power and laid back on the planks, again absorbed by the painted figures and clouds and sky. Darby didn't know what to say to the boy, or to Arthur. The kid had remained for the rest of the previous day, though by his own admission he had little to contribute. Darby had retreated into himself, anger filling him from all directions, though mostly at Arthur. Couldn't fault James as much, Arthur's charity a subtle but immoveable force no one could argue against. Darby had spent a good portion of the previous evening in a repetitive cycle, powering up his phone, opening Arthur's contact information, and powering down again.

"Can I stay up here today?" James' voice bounced down from the vaulted ceiling.

"Up to you," Darby said.

"I like it. Peaceful."

Darby removed his coat, shivered at the temperature shift, and tied his canvas apron around his waist. His hands moved hard, jerking the straps into a rough bow, like they could tear the straps out of the apron on his behalf. He climbed the ladder and prepared his palette for the morning's work, scooping paint hard enough to make it spatter onto his apron. Mostly gold for the fringed highlights on the north-oriented gargoyle's ears.

"You're mad," James said.

"Arthur must've needed to have you working."

"I called him last night. Told him about yesterday."

Which I couldn't do, Darby thought. The kid sounded so matter-of-fact.

"And?"

"He said not to worry about it. Said you go way back."

"We do."

"That you'd understand. About me."

"I don't, not really. And I do. Shit."

The last time Darby he been so angry he had a six-inch hole through his side and shrapnel embedded in his hip and Arthur had already administered last rites. A small corvette had gotten through the naval blockade and lobbed an antipersonnel shell at the airfield, airbursting over the mess tent, pulping a dozen men into ribbons of simple meat and shards of splintered bone. A stray fragment scything through Darby as he sheltered a few hundred yards away under the Sabre jet he'd been working on. Nose art commissioned by the crew—they always got Darby to do the work—as a gift to the pilot. BROADWAY in garish yellows and reds under a misproportioned showgirl. The pain a universe. The chaplain moved like a spirit between dead and dying men but still found time to hold Darby's hand when the morphine ran out. He was surprised to find Darby alive hours later on the flight line waiting to be evac'ed to the surgical unit farther south. Slipped a card with his home address into Darby's blood-stained tunic, the other hand steady and warm on his shoulder.

"Still cold up here," James said.

"Winter's like that."

"Heater takes longer than you'd think it would."

Darby cracked his knuckles and picked up his brush, mixing a tiny dab of titanium white into the gold, digging it in. The opacity of the white bringing out the flecks of colour. Less prone to yellowing, too. Keep the layers purer longer, Darby figured.

Some time later, James's voice brought Darby forward. He sat back, stretched his shoulders and back, and breathed in, satisfied. It felt good to dial himself in so thoroughly again, the kid's presence for the past couple days an itch just under the veneer of his concentration. Enough to forget about the temperature and his stiffness for a short time, the scars, that tiny piece of iron that the surgeons couldn't get out of the pelvic bone. Some of the anger had gone, too, bled away like heat across a winter's day, or steam from a long, slow breath.

"What?"

"I asked how come you never ask," James said.

"About what?"

"Afghanistan."

"Why would I?"

"Arthur told me you know."

"I don't share my stories, so I don't ask for others'."

"I never know who'll ask."

"People don't really know how, in my experience."

"Kids're the worst. 'You see anyone die?' 'You kill anyone?' 'Was it fun?' God, their questions."

"Honest, at least."

"Yeah. But you can't say much."

Nor should you, Darby thought.

"You could still do some work," he said after a moment. "Filling in, or something."

"Maybe later. Have to disappear for a bit."

"Now?"

"My joints are starting to seize up anyhow."

"They'll do that."

James moved towards the ladder at the sides of the scaffolding, the planks bowing under his weight, and went down. Heavy for his height and frame, Darby noticed for the first time. Carried some muscle. He watched as the kid crossed the floor, stretched, and bouncing on the balls of his feet, muttering under his breath, the sound strange, whispery echoes in the vast space. Darby covered the palette and waited, only descending after the heavy outer doors closed with a shudder. Decided to go for a walk to warm up.

Arthur was on the step when Darby shouldered open the heavy doors, savouring a fat, dark cigar, his back to the church, facing the city. No coughing, no talking. Just watching. A kind of visible peace, even from behind, a rare thing. Darby sighed, not finding it in himself to resurrect the anger he'd intended to direct towards Arthur's mistruth about the boy. The priest's head turned slightly at the sound.

"Guess I'm busted."

"Into confession with you, young man," Darby said.

"A sinner I am, I am, I am …"

Arthur sang the line. Low. He'd always carried a nice baritone.

"Don't know that one," Darby said.

"Made it up for some girl."

"Uh huh."

"Before all of this—" Arthur pointed across his throat then swept his hands down his body, ghost shapes of dog collar and vestments. "A long time ago, of course."

"Sure, sure."

"You probably thought I made it up for you. Right now."

Arthur laughed at his own joke, coughed his way clear. Handkerchief out again to catch whatever unholiness he brought up from his lungs. Darby always watched for a bloom of red to appear, as in the movies. He laid a hand on Arthur's shoulder, his friend leaning towards it slightly, as though it was a new sort of weight to bear.

"So my secret is out," Arthur said.

"Not much of one—smell of smoke's hard to hide."

"Don't tell anyone."

"Who the hell would I tell?"

Arthur gave a shrug. "The docs aren't keen on it," he said.

"Oh, but I'm sure you never inhale."

"Ha! They'd probably believe *you*—"

"*Woe to the fool who utters falsehood on behalf of guilty men …*"

"Made that one up, I'm sure."

Just as Darby was about to respond in kind, that he'd conjured the awkward proverb right then, a shadow flitted dark across his mood. He removed his hand. Arthur noticed, half-turned towards him.

"What's wrong?"

"You told me he was an artist," Darby said.

"Oh, that."

"'Oh, that.' Christ. I'm calling foul play."

"You're not paying him."

"That's not the point. Why'd you lie to me?"

"No skin off your nose at all. In fact—"

Arthur reached into his pocket and took out an envelope. Handed it to Darby.

"What's this for?"

"James. It's his last day."

"Wait—"

"I couldn't catch him when he left. Can you give it to him?"

"But he hasn't actually done anything!"

Arthur winced and opened his mouth as if to say something, closed it again. Took a long haul on the cigar instead, then exhaled. He scrutinized the tube of ash at the tip for a moment before blowing on it. The ash disintegrated, exposing the cherry, which brightened then dimmed to grey.

"Corporate called me this morning," Arthur said. "They won't give an extension."

"I need at least an extra week to—"

"—get it done right, yeah, I know. You'll just have to do what you can. The place already looks a million times better."

"It'll stand out if I don't finish. "

"At least you'll get paid."

Darby snorted. "The kid, too."

"We help our own."

"He's a goddamned fake."

Arthur looked at Darby a long moment and shook his head. "He'll find the art somewhere."

"He admitted it to me, Arthur."

"Just give the envelope to him. Should be enough."

"Look at me—"

But the priest wouldn't. He mumbled a goodbye, walked down the steps, and turned left, north along the sidewalk, striking up a soundtrack of coughs. Darby watched his back, too stunned to move. He had the brief but powerful urge to stuff the envelope in his coat and never mention it. Use it for himself. No one to say he couldn't. The perfect, passive rebuttal for the anger his friend was making him feel. His word against the kid's, a chance to be as stubborn about the truth as anyone else. But—

"Jesus, look at you. Gotta get you to the heater," James said, appearing from nowhere. A tray with two beverages from Tim Horton's in his right hand, a box-strained Canadian Tire bag in the other. The bag translucent white.

"No."

"Your lips are blue, sir."

"I can't."

"Come on—cold as fuck out here."

"I'm fine. I'll be in in a moment."

"Brought drinks—"

"I see that."

"Coffee."

"Jesus, kid. I don't—"

"Their tea is shit anyhow."

With a chuckle, James tucked the box under his arm, moved past Darby, reaching for the worn brass handles on the door. As the huge doors opened, there was the brush of weather-stripping across stone, the hush of displaced air. Enough to puff out the bag and reveal the side of the box. A photograph of an electric kettle in stainless steel and black plastic. A gift, maybe. What to do with such a thing. As James held open the door, Darby walked into the church, sliding the envelope into his rear pants pocket. Wondering what he might say to the boy.

ACKNOWLEDGEMENTS

Storytelling is the great unifier, humanity's truly collective art, and the standard-bearer for our highest truths. Thank you for reading my stories. I'm grateful to all the story-makers in my life, from Mom and Dad who read to me at bedtime to the incredible writers I admire and read now, many of whom I'm privileged to call my friends. Thanks to Michael Mirolla and everyone at Guernica Editions for this gorgeous collection. Thanks to the journal and magazine editors who've championed my work along the way: seeing my words in print is a thrill, but knowing they're being read is the true honour. Special thanks to BSSP's Joe Melia and TNQ's Pamela Mulloy and Susan Scott, champions of the emerging writer and all-around good people. Public support for the arts is vital, and I'm humbled by the financial aid I've received from the Canada Council for the Arts, the Ontario Arts Council, and the Hamilton Arts Council. Thanks to the teachers and students who've pushed my craft to new heights, particularly the gifted souls in the UBC creative writing program. For their inspiration, lessons, and patience with me, cheers to Hugh Cook, Steph Vandermeulen, Liz Harmer, Amanda

Leduc, Andrew Forbes, Kevin Hardcastle, Colette Maitland, Ellen Keith, Carly Vandergriendt, JR McConvey, Michael Winter, Saleema Nawaz, Madeleine Thien, SFS InkWells, HPL, and the host of others I've undoubtedly forgotten. To RELAY Coffee, the best writer-fuel around. Thanks to God the Creator, the original storyweaver, for this gift. Thanks to my sibs and sibs-in-law, and all their kids. To my girls Nora and Alida, whose pure love of stories is a daily reminder of how vital they are. And finally, as ever, my eternal gratitude to my wife Rosalee, who encourages, pushes, and loves me towards every story I tell. I love you.

STORY NOTABLES:

"Skinks" was the winner of the Fiddlehead Best Short Story Prize and was published in *The Fiddlehead* and *The Advent Short Story Calendar*.

"Drift, Maybe Fall" was the winner of the Lush Triumphant Literary Award and was published in *subTerrain*.

"Qom" was longlisted for the CBC Short Story Award and was published in *EVENT*.

"Cut Road" was published in *Riddle Fence* and was nominated for the Journey Prize.

"Bayfront" was published in *The New Quarterly*.

"A Week on the Water" won the Bristol Short Story Prize and was published in the contest anthology.

"Pieces of Echo" was the winner of the Our Darkest Hours Prize and was published in *The Writer Magazine*.

"Mom 2 Mom" was published in *The Dalhousie Review*.

"Fairly Traded" was an honourable mention for the Peter Hinchcliffe Fiction Award and was published in *The New Quarterly*.

"Those Days Just a Glimmer" was the winner of the Freda Waldon Award for Fiction and was published in *The Fiddlehead*.

"Declination" was published in *The Prairie Review* and was nominated for the Journey Prize.

"Barton Walkup" was published in *Prairie Fire*.

"The Echoes Are All Mine" was published in *The New Quarterly* and was longlisted for the CBC Short Story Prize and the CVC/Exile Short story Award.

"Buddy's Mirror" was published in *The New Guard Literary Review* and was a finalist in the Machigonne Fiction Contest.

ABOUT THE AUTHOR

Brent van Staalduinen is a former high school English teacher, army medic, radio announcer, and tree planter, and is the author of the novels *Nothing But Life* (shortlisted for the 2022 White Pine Award), *Boy* (winner of the 2021 Kerry Schooley Book Award), and *Saints, Unexpected*. His short stories have won numerous awards and have been published in journals on both sides of the Atlantic. *Cut Road* is his first collection. He lives in Hamilton, Ontario with his wife Rosalee and daughters Nora and Alida.

For more information about Brent and his writing, visit www.brentvans.com and follow him on Twitter, Facebook, and Instagram (@brentvans).